Maggie noticed that the hands that helped her sit upright were careful to be gentle.

Big, coarse hands, the sunburned hands of a farmer. Handsome hands, in their own way. She blushed when he caught her staring.

"Well, thanks for bringing over the tea. I think I can manage the rest."

But, as she was weak as a kitten, the steaming cup shook so much in Maggie's hand that she was forced to accept Rafe's help. His know-it-all smile was so maddening that she found it hard to be gracious. She was annoyed, too, that he smelled so soapy clean and she felt so grungy. Hated that when he bent his head, his silky, black hair brushed her forehead, and was soft and smelled of pine trees.

But she hated *most* that when he held up the cup of sweet, fragrant tea, his hand grazed her lips. She was glad that her falling hair hid the rush of heat that stained her cheeks.

Dear Reader,

My mother always told me that if you had a full tank of gas, you were never lost. Would that our heroine knew that. On a rainswept night, low on gas and sneezing her way into the flu...can any good come of this? Well...

Adventures can happen any time, the world is full of surprises, and Mother Nature cares not if, like our heroine, your nose is red, your eyes are bleary, and you're not exactly at your best in…um…those sweats you've been wearing since the beginning of time. It's all about seizing the moment.

I first met my husband when I was running to take a final exam. We literally bumped into each other on a staircase, apologized profusely, and hurried on. I didn't see him again for three months—but I was watching for him all over campus! The next time I saw him, I promise you, I walked more slowly. Forty years later, I still remember what he was wearing that first night.

Did we make the moment, or did the moment make us? When Fate comes knocking on our door, we answer, but that is not always enough. Sometimes we have to go the extra mile to make things work. Scary? Sure it is, but it's all part of the adventure.

Happy reading!

Barbara Gale

THE FARMER TAKES A WIFE

BARBARA GALE

SPECIAL EDITION

Published by Silhouette Books

America's Publisher of Contemporary Romance

For my dad, Louis Rubinstein,
who would have enjoyed hiking on Rafe's mountain.

 SILHOUETTE BOOKS

ISBN-13: 978-0-373-24852-0
ISBN-10:   0-373-24852-0

THE FARMER TAKES A WIFE

Copyright © 2007 by Barbara Einstein

Visit Silhouette Books at www.eHarlequin.com

Printed in U.S.A.

Books by Barbara Gale

Special Edition

The Ambassador's Vow #1500
Down from the Mountain #1595
Picking Up the Pieces #1674
Finding His Way Home #1812
The Farmer Takes a Wife #1852

BARBARA GALE

is a native New Yorker. Married for over thirty years, she, her husband and their three children divide their time between Brooklyn and Hobart, New York. Barbara has always been fascinated with the implications of outside factors, including race, on relationships. She knows that love is as powerful as romance readers believe it is.

She loves to hear from readers. Write to her at P.O. Box 150792, Brooklyn, New York 11215-0792 or Barbara@BarbaraGale.com, and visit her Web site at www.barbaragale.com.

The Ladies' Best Homemade Apple Pie
as sold at the Primrose Farmers' Market

2 deep dish pie shells (frozen or homemade)
1 egg white, slightly beaten
5 tart peeled apples, thinly sliced
1-¼ cups sugar
2 tbsps flour
2 tsps cinnamon
1 tbsp lemon juice
4 tbsps butter, chopped

Preheat oven to 450°F.
Place one shell in deep dish pie plate. Coat shell with egg white; remove and save excess.
Defrost pie shells, if necessary.
Peel, slice apples, and coat slices with lemon juice.

Mix in large mixing bowl:

1 cup sugar
2 tbsps flour
½ tsp cinnamon

Coat apples with sugar mixture and place in pie shell.
Scatter chopped butter over apple filling.
Cover pie with second pie shell. Gently seal edges together; gently slash four steam holes in the pie shell cover.
Brush shell with remaining egg white.
Sprinkle with sugar/cinnamon mix (remaining ¼ cup sugar and 1 tsp cinnamon).
Place pie in oven on top of tinfoil or baking sheet.
Bake pie at 450°F for 10 minutes, then reduce heat to 350°F and bake 45 minutes longer.

Chapter One

A town is saved, not more by the righteous men in it, than by the woods and swamps that surround it.
—Henry David Thoreau, 1862

Her windshield wipers on high, Maggie tried not to panic as she nudged her van closer to the shoulder of the road, struggling to keep to the narrow mountain pass. Using cuss words she didn't know she knew, she swore in no uncertain terms that this trip was definitely going to be her last. She was getting too old for this nonsense. Let the younger doctors do it. A hair-raising drive through the rain-swept mountains of New Hampshire was *not* her idea of a good time, even if it was July. As a roving doctor for the Mobile Clinic of New England, Maggie had long accepted that getting lost was a part of the job, and usually saw it as an adventure. But her adventures usually took place in Massachusetts, where she lived. She had only offered to do the New Hampshire route as a favor to a sick friend. Not that the last two weeks hadn't been wonderful. It had been easy to fall in love with New Hampshire and the White Mountains, and the wonderful people who had taken her into their homes and hearts. But in this moment, nursing a cold and running a fever, she was in no mood to explore another country lane. Lost in the mountains in the middle of a major thunderstorm, no cell phone reception, her thermos empty and her gas tank not far behind… Cuss words were the least of her problems.

Well, there was a lesson to be learned. From now on, she would definitely pay more attention to the weather report, as she would have done if she hadn't been so anxious to get back home and nurse her wretched cold. The thought of crawling into bed with a box of tissues had been so compelling she'd ignored her common sense. And to make matters worse, *if that were possible*, her sneezes were coming on fast and furious, she was running low on tissue, and—doctor that she was—there wasn't a single cold pill in her black bag! Oh, if only she had followed her instincts and made that U-turn four miles back! On the other hand, if she didn't find a gas station pretty soon she wouldn't be making *any* turns. She supposed she *could* pull over and sleep in back of the van until someone found her. Surely the state police patrolled these roads. No question, a tall, handsome trooper was just what she needed.

No, a trooper *and* a cup of hot tea.

Actually, the way she was feeling, she could skip the trooper.

Maggie was fighting a migraine when her luck finally turned. Squinting hard, she was sure her feverish eyes had caught a glimpse of something. *Yesss!* Obscured by shrubbery and barely discernable through the relentless sheet of gray rain, but yes, that *was* a sign propped against a low-limbed tree, its post long since rotted. The white paint was peeling, and half the letters were missing. Nevertheless, it was a road sign, and with it, the promise of civilization. Please God, let it say Bloomville, the way her map promised.

Pr m se
P p. 350
3 il s

Promise? It certainly did not *say Bloomville*. It was a pity she was not more familiar with New Hampshire.

Pop. 350 Tiny.

3 ils. Was that *three* miles, or *thirty* miles? Glancing at her gas gauge, Maggie prayed it was only three, as she pointed her van in the direction of the sign.

Ten more minutes later, barely able to sketch the lone, battered gas pump just visible through the pouring rain, she pulled into a gas station, her relief almost palpable. That last clap of thunder had sent her heart thumping so wildly she didn't even care whether the gas pump was operable, if only another human being was around to offer her company. Leaning across the console to peer out the passenger window, she fought the sense of unreality that met her eyes. *Murky and desolate* did not bode well for a hot cup of tea. Hopefully the scruffy OPEN sign dangling from the door didn't lie, because the dark window of the store looming past the pump was no shimmering invitation to travelers. Everything about the place said *uninhabited*, even if the sign said otherwise. Well, welcomed or not, this was one stop she wasn't going to pass up. Grabbing her bag, Maggie left the shelter of the van to dash through the summer storm.

"Helloanybodyhome?" Knocking on the door of the tiny store was a given, calling out *hello* was an act of faith. Hopefully, someone would hear past the drumming of the rain. Not surprised when no one answered, Maggie jiggled the door knob, relieved when it gave way. Maybe the *OPEN* sign was for real, but the musty odor that greeted her was a message of stale disuse. She was careful to remain just within the doorway, until she was sure of her safety. Traveling as she did, she had a great many rules in place. Even from a distance, she could tell that the meager supply of shelved merchandise was coated with a thin layer of dust. Littered with yellow newspapers, a narrow Formica counter skirted the

far side of the shop. A hundred years of soda cans were crammed into a large garbage can, the only evidence of any attempt at order. Her heart rebelled against the lack of sanitation, the sight more unnerving than fear for her safety. Boldly, she flipped a nearby light switch, grateful when it lit the drab store, even if it didn't do it all that well.

"Helloanybodyhome?" she called again. Surely *somebody* must live there. Idly, she checked the expiration date of a bag of peanuts resting on a rusty metal rack. The crackle of foil was apparently more effective than her shouts.

"I assume you plan to pay for that."

Startled, Maggie turned to see an elderly, thickset woman materialize from behind a ragged green curtain that may have once been velvet. A heavy gray braid haloed the crown of her head, her hollow eyes were brown pebbles in a pasty face that hadn't seen fresh air in months.

"Hi," Maggie said, managing a polite smile. "I was just passing through and stopped for gas. Well, passing through might be a bit of an overstatement. I think I'm lost."

"You *think* you're lost?" the old woman repeated, her gravelly voice mocking.

Maggie's answer was a light, singsong laugh. "Okay, yes, I'm pretty sure I'm lost. I was heading home to Boston, and took a wrong turn, but the way it's raining, I was glad to find this place. I was trying to find a town called Bloomville and maybe spend the night there, but this isn't Bloomville, is it?" she said, looking about her. "I think the sign I passed a mile back might have said *Promise*, but I'm not entirely sure. I don't know New Hampshire all that well."

"It's Primrose," the woman snapped. "No promise here," she snorted.

Not *precisely* hostile, Maggie consoled herself as she watched the old woman shuffle slowly toward the counter. Relying heavily on a cane for support, she was doing a bad job of hiding her pain, wincing as she settled herself in an old rocker. As a doctor, Maggie's heart went out to her, but she knew better than to say. "I'd like to fill up. I honked, but no one answered."

"Well, it says *self serve* so that may be why," the woman said dryly. "Besides, these old legs stopped serving gas a long time ago. I've only got *high test*, though, missy. Sold the last of the *regular* last week. But seeing as how I'm the only gas station this side of the mountain, I guess you'll take it."

"And be glad of it," Maggie said, unfazed by the woman's prickly humor. "Am I right in assuming that you're the owner of this gas station?"

"No other reason to be here," the woman said tartly as she propped her feet on a stool. From the corner of her eye, Maggie noticed that although they were wrapped, almost *bound*, in heavy stockings, the swell of the old woman's ankles could not be disguised. She must be in terrific pain, Maggie thought, but an unlikely candidate for sympathy, if the proud look in her eyes was any indication.

"Well, then, if you don't mind, I think I'll go fill up."

"I don't mind. And I won't forget to add the price of those peanuts you're holding, neither."

I bet you don't, Maggie sighed, shoving the bag of peanuts in her pocket as she dashed back into the storm. Her hoodie totally inadequate, she bowed her head against the cold, wet rain and ran to the pumps, fighting a sudden onset of sneezes. If she didn't dry off soon, she was sure to wake up with pneumonia—that is, if she was lucky enough to find a bed.

Filling her tank as the rain beat down on her shoulders, the prickly feeling on Maggie's neck told her the old woman was watching her every move, although what she could possibly see through those filthy windows was beyond Maggie. Maggie herself could hardly read the pump gauge for the downpour, and she was standing right beside it. Returning to the store on the edge of a piercing clap of thunder, she shook herself free of the rain and rummaged about in her bag for some tissue. Now, not only was her nose running, but her hair was a wet mop. "It *is* wet out there, isn't it?" she laughed.

Undeterred by the woman's lack of response, she plowed on. "You know, I'd be as glad of a hot meal as much as for that gas. If you could direct me to the nearest restaurant, I'd be grateful."

A disapproving look clouding her eyes, the old woman ignored Maggie's question. "I see you're driving one of the New England medical vans."

"Yes…yes, I am. I'm surprised you could read the words through the rain."

"My eyesight ain't gone yet, missy."

Okaaay. Maggie tried for polite. "Are you part of the county circuit?"

"Mayhaps. We're supposed to be part of the Bloomville Township circuit. When they remember us, that is," the woman snorted. "Bloomville is way over on the other side of the mountain. I guess it's hard to see for the trees," she said acerbically.

Maggie almost laughed but caught herself in time. The woman might be cranky but she did seem to have a sense of humor. "Sounds like you make use of the Mobile Medical Van."

"We do, when it shows up!"

Maggie frowned to hear an accusation hanging in the air. "Are you saying that the van missed an appointment?"

"That's *exactly* what I'm saying! It was supposed to be here last April but it never showed."

Uh oh, so *that's* what this was all about. And it was quite clear who was going to take the blame for the *no show*. "Ma'am, if the van never showed, I honestly wouldn't know why. My own route usually keeps me in Massachusetts. I'm doing New Hampshire this month, for a friend. Did you call to ask what happened?"

"Of course I did, but I got the usual runaround. No one knew, said they'd investigate…blah…blah… blah."

Maggie was taken aback. "They're usually pretty good about those things. How about if I make some calls…when I'm back on my feet, I mean. I seem to have come down with the most god-awful cold."

If the woman didn't notice how sick she was, she did when Maggie went off into a spasm of sneezes. Retrieving a soggy wad of tissues from her pocket, Maggie blew her nose so loudly she sounded like a foghorn. Not that the old woman probably cared. She seemed more concerned with the absence of the medical van than extending Maggie any hospitality. Given the shape her feet were in, Maggie didn't blame her. But she herself wasn't in good shape, either.

"Look, ma'am," Maggie explained on another nasally honk. "I guess I made a wrong turn some-where, probably more than one," she admitted grimly, "but at this point I have no choice but to find a motel. So, if you could point the way, the nearest one will do."

"Gas…food…a motel room…" the old woman muttered. "I doubt I remember the last time we had a visitor, these parts."

I can't imagine why. But clenching her teeth, Maggie forced a determined smile. "That doesn't bode well for me."

"No, it doesn't," the old lady agreed, not an ounce of sympathy in her shrewd, rheumy eyes.

Chilled to the bone and feeling downright mis-erable, Maggie wanted a motel room badly, a dry bed on which to lay her aching head. She most certainly did not want to be stalled, which she suspected the old woman was doing—and thoroughly enjoying herself in the process. On the other hand, she didn't want to alienate the one person who could point the way to a safe haven, if she so chose. Worse came to worst, Maggie supposed she *could* sleep in her van, but an uneasy glance out the window said that *would* be a worst-case scenario. It might be July, but it was pouring cats and dogs outside, and besides, sleeping in a van filled with medical supplies would be uncomfortable, not to mention cold. Not that she hadn't slept in a car before, but she was seventeen at the time, and Tommy Lee had been a mighty warm blanket, and— Relinquishing the hope of a hot cup of tea, she pleaded her case one more time. "Look, ma'am—"

"The name is Louisa Haymaker. *Ma'am* makes me sound old."

"*Mrs. Haymaker*, then," Maggie apologized, feeling like Alice in Wonderland. "I'm cold and wet, tired and hungry. I wouldn't be surprised if I'm coming down with pneumonia. All things combined, I can't possibly drive another mile. Surely there must be *someplace* around here I can stay. If credentials help…" Maggie hated to put herself forward, she hardly ever did, but this seemed an excellent time to trade on her position. Shifting her huge leather tote, she rummaged through her belongings until she pulled out a stethoscope, better than any business card, and dangled it in the air. "Did I mention that I was a doctor? Does that get me any points?"

Finally, a flicker of interest in those rheumy, old

eyes! Flashing her Boston Mercy Hospital ID, Maggie rushed on. "Look, Mrs. Haymaker, my name is Doctor Margaret Tremont. I'm not feeling too well and I just want to go home, but since I can't, I want a hotel." Catching her breath, Maggie placed a twenty dollar bill on the counter. "I don't think I paid you for the gas."

Snakelike, Louisa Haymaker's hand shot out to pocket the money. Maggie noticed she didn't bother to offer any change. "And the name of a motel? If you could recommend one, I would be on my way."

But whatever help Louisa Haymaker might have offered was interrupted by the unexpected crashing of the rickety screen door, which made them both jump. Shoulders hunched against the wind, a small boy rushed in, bringing with him violent gusts of cold air until he managed to slam shut the door.

"Louisa, where are you? We're heeere!" The boy's cheerful greeting in the face of the thunderstorm was heartwarming, and his careless trail of rainwater made Maggie smile, but it did nothing for Louisa Haymaker's temper.

"Amos Burnside, how many times do I have to tell you not to slam that door! If it falls down—no, *when* it falls down—who's going to fix it, I'd like to know? Just look at the mess you're making!" she croaked, pointing with her cane at the water pooling at his feet.

Chagrined, the little boy looked down at the puddle his boots had made. The way his baseball hat covered his face, it was hard to tell, but Maggie wondered if he was about to cry. She judged him to about seven or eight years old, and his soft, high-pitched voice told her she was right.

"Louisa," he protested. "I can't help it if it's raining."

"Fine! You're right, child. Look, we have a guest."

Amos followed the direction of Louisa's eyes. Shocked to see a stranger, he tugged free his hat to get a better look, startling Maggie with his head of silky, corn yellow hair.

"Who are you?" he asked, his shimmering blue eyes wide with surprise.

Surprised by his ethereal beauty, Maggie wondered who was responsible for this angel in desperate need of a haircut. "My name is Margaret Tremont," she explained between two violent sneezes into the last of her dusty tissues. "But my friends call me Maggie."

"You sure sneeze loud," he said gravely.

"She's sick, can't you tell?" Louisa scolded him. "Young miss stopped for gas. *She says she's a doctor.*"

Amos' smile was an engaging confection of pure pleasure and unabashed curiosity. "*Really?* An honest-to-goodness real doctor?"

"Honest-to-goodness," Maggie promised with a watery smile.

"Wow! Wait till I tell dad! I'm Amos Burnside, but my friends call me Amos," he said with artless candor.

"Glad to meet you, Amos," Maggie rasped. "Uh oh, I think I'm starting to lose my voice."

"Louisa's right, you *do* sound sick. If you're a real doctor why don't you make yourself better?"

"Amos, if I knew how to cure the common cold, I'd not only feel better, I'd be a rich woman."

"My dad says that too, every time *I* get a cold! If *I* knew how to cure a cold would I be rich?"

"The richest boy on earth, my friend."

"Well, then, maybe that's what I'll do when I grow up!"

My hat's off to you, kid, Maggie murmured to herself. *And if you could manage to do it by tomorrow, I would be grateful.*

But Amos had moved on to new territory, in the way that children did. In one sentence, or less.

"WhatareyoudoinghereDoctortremontissomeone-sickhowlongareyoustayingitsnotsafetodriveatnight-intherainmydadsaysso—"

"Whoa, young man! That's a lot of questions. Well, let's see. No one is sick here that I know of—except me," she explained with a small laugh. "I was on my way home—I live in Boston—when I got caught in the storm and stumbled into Mrs. Haymaker's gas station. My good luck because I was nearly out of gas. I would be glad, as well, to stumble into a warm bed with a box of tissues! As a matter of fact, I was just asking Mrs. Haymaker directions to the nearest motel when you arrived."

Amos turned to Louisa with a puzzled look. "Louisa, why didn't you tell her about the cabins out back? Sorry, doctor, Louisa must have forgot because we don't get many visitors to Primrose." Amos smiled as if it were his fault. "You must have missed the sign."

"I seem to have missed many signs," Maggie said, sending Louisa a flinty look.

"Louisa owns the motel out back. It's called *Jack's Haven*, after Louisa's husband, Mr. Jack, except he's not her husband anymore because he's dead, but he *would* be her husband if he were still alive. Wouldn't he, Louisa?"

"Amos Burnside," Louisa said, cool as a cucumber, "you know as well as anyone those cabins are unfit to rent. Cold as all get out, and damp, to boot," she told Maggie firmly. "If you're sick, you'll want a better place to stay, somewhere warm, where the roof isn't about to fall on your head."

"Louisa, the roof isn't going to fall down! Dad patched them just last week," the boy reminded her. "Don't you remember? I helped! And anyway, there is no other place to stay. If it really is that cold in the cabins, I'll be glad to help you build a fire. Dad taught me how to do it last weekend when he took me camping and—"

If looks could kill, Amos would have been a photo in the old woman's memory box, but there was nothing Louisa could do to stop the boy talking without embarrassing them both.

"I'd be glad to build you a fire, Doctor Tremont," Amos promised Maggie with an earnest smile.

Biting her lip to keep from smiling, Maggie was all grave politeness. "Thank you, Amos. I would be grateful for your help." *Good lord, from what cloud had this child fallen?*

"Well…" Louisa hesitated, but knew she had no choice. Maggie must be allowed to stay, unless Louisa wanted to make a scene. "I suppose it would be all right…for just one night."

Maggie didn't like that timeline, but if her foot was in the door, she would not ask for more. "Thank you, Mrs. Haymaker. The idea of driving to Bloomville was daunting, and the thought of sleeping in my car was…um…alarming."

Amos was impressed. "You drove all the way from Bloomville?"

"No, I got lost *looking* for Bloomville," Maggie explained. "I know from my map that Bloomville is not that far, only fifty miles or so, but with all the rain, I could hardly see the signs."

"It's far enough that *I've* only been there once," Amos said mournfully.

"But how could that be?" Maggie asked with surprise. "It's only on the other side of the mountain."

"My dad goes once in a while, on an emergency, and to get groceries and stuff, but he never lets me go with him. He says there's nothing there, that we have everything we want here at home. Rafe says—"

"Who is *Rafe?*" Maggie asked.

"Rafe is my dad. Sometimes I call him dad, and sometimes I call him Rafe. He's getting Louisa's groceries out of the truck. Rafe says that people who leave home sometimes lose their way back. Like my mom. She left when I was a baby and we never saw her again. Rafe says—"

"Amos!" Louisa snapped, visibly alarmed at the boy's indiscretions. "I don't think—"

But before Louisa could explain further, the door swung wide and a rain-drenched man strode through the door, bringing with him the scent of wet leaves and damp wool. Tall as he was broad, he moved with grace as he slammed shut the door with his boot heel, his arms balancing three brown bags filled to overflowing with groceries.

"Amos," the man said, his voice admonishing yet gentle at the same time, "you sure did disappear in a hurry. You were supposed to see if Louisa was awake, then come back and help me with these groceries."

Maggie was intrigued by the low timbre of the gentle voice that still managed to sound stern. But whereas Amos Burnside was a ray of sunlight on this dreary, gray day, his father—it could be no other— was a rough caricature of beauty, his weather-beaten face a maze of deep creases and a day-old beard beneath a battered gray, felt hat.

And Maggie could not stop looking.

A silky black curtain, his long, dark hair clung damply to his forehead. His eyes were black coals beneath a thick, black brow. His nose was strong and straight, and a square jutting jaw lent him a sensual, masculine air. If his stained denim jeans and mud-splattered work boots weren't enough evidence of a life led outdoors, his bulky plaid jacket added to the impression. But it was the size of him that was most remarkable. Standing at about six feet two, and maybe half as wide, he was one of those men who insinuated with pure, male presence. Maggie guessed there was probably no space he wouldn't dominate.

Something in the air must have revealed her presence because, suddenly on the alert, Rafe turned in her direction, still clutching the brown bags. Finding her, his eyes grew wide and he fixed her with a searching look, his demeanor changing with his discovery. His fierce frown didn't help to disguise his annoyance, either. Maggie tried to smile, but he wasn't buying into it. Watching his mouth work itself into a thin line of displeasure, she felt herself flush with embarrassment. But it was too late. She was a butterfly pinned by a single glance from his piercing blue eyes. Eyes that were at once outraged, contemptuous, and yet…revealed a concentration of interest. Surely it was the same look that Adam sent Eve when he stumbled on her for the first time.

Maggie's immediate impression was that no happiness lived here, that the sway of Rafe's shoulders was too stiff, that something about this man said he had aged too quickly. Maybe it was the way he moved…slowly…as if it took great effort—not precisely a careless restraint, but perhaps a result of indifference. But something told Maggie that where this man stood had once been beauty—happiness, too, maybe—even if it were only the vaguest shadow dance, now. Maggie marveled that she saw so much at once, and dismissed herself as fanciful. No doubt it was the reason her breath had caught in her lungs.

Chapter Two

Somebody took a wrong turn somewhere, Rafe decided grimly as he set the grocery bags down on the counter and stared boldly at the woman holding up the wall. Late thirties, if he guessed right. Sickly, too, if he were any judge of red noses, chapped lips and rashy cheeks. Of course, the wet weather could account for that, but the lady did look a sorry mess. He had no idea who she was, had no idea why she was there, but he did know one thing: the town of Primrose *never* entertained.

"What's going on here?" he asked, his voice soft. But nobody—not the adults, in any case—could fail to perceive his underlying displeasure.

"Hey, Dad, this here is Maggie Tremont," Amos

announced, excited beyond anything to be the bearer of news. And such news! A stranger invading Shangri-la could not have been more exotic to his young eyes. "She's lost, Dad! And guess what? She's a *doctor*, no kidding!"

Maggie watched as Rafe reassessed her through the filter of this new information. No matter—she could have been the Queen of Sheba—she knew what he saw was unimpressive. When people said your nose was your best asset, you knew your mirror didn't lie. If her gray eyes sparkled when she laughed, she knew nothing about *that*. And though her skin would never be radiant there was something to be said for a smattering of freckles and pink cheeks, even if they were a bit feverish just at the moment. If something in Rafe's eyes made her regret her lack of beauty, Maggie tamped down her unexpected reaction as quickly as it rose. Her confidence in her abilities was too finely rooted to be influenced by a sour glance from a man, even if he did have broad shoulders.

Vaguely, she listened as Louisa explained her arrival to Rafe. It was vexing, the way they talked as if she weren't there, but feeling queasy, she did not interfere. Common sense told her to mind her manners. She had a feeling that being snappish wouldn't get her anywhere with this pair. But containing her irritation wasn't easy, the way her head was throbbing. Couldn't they see how sick she was and that she only wanted a bed?

"Yes, my name really is Doctor Margaret

Tremont," she said wearily. "I'm one of the small crew of doctors who work for the Mobile Clinic of New England."

Rafe studied her thoughtfully. "We use their services, but our association is with a Doctor Marks."

"Yes, I know him, he's a great guy, and don't worry, I'm not his replacement. Listen, I don't even belong here in New Hampshire. I work the Massachusetts corridor because I live in Boston. Technically, I'm not even on duty! I mean, there I was on 93 South, and then...I wasn't!" she sighed.

Rafe's look was disparaging. "I know the highway wanders when you cross the state line, but not *that* much."

"Enough to lose my way," Maggie said ruefully, wondering if getting lost was a cardinal sin in these parts. "Like I said, I'm unfamiliar with this area. I passed Concord hours ago. But give me a month and I'll be able to tell you all the landmarks. I have a very good sense of direction...usually," she declared with a light laugh.

Rafe was skeptical. "You've strayed pretty far from home for someone with a good sense of direction. Boston is miles south of here."

"Isn't that the truth?" Maggie smiled wryly. "Somewhere, somehow, I took a wrong turn—*majorly!* There were a few moments when I was absolutely petrified I'd fall off the side of the mountain. Right about when the asphalt turned to mud. If I were you, I'd call the department of highways and complain."

"What makes you think we haven't?" Rafe asked coldly.

Maggie was startled by his sudden flash of temper. "Yes, I guess you would have," she said diplomatically. "Well, lucky for me I saw that sign for Primrose. It led me here. Mrs. Haymaker was just about to offer me a room for the night when Amos appeared—*weren't you*, Mrs. Haymaker?"

Maggie held her breath, hoping Mrs. Haymaker's sense of justice would come to her aid. If she didn't find a bed in the next five minutes, she was going to collapse on Louisa's mucky linoleum floor. Quickly, she moved to the Formica counter and rummaged about in her bag for her checkbook. "Is a hundred dollars for the night fair market value, Mrs. Haymaker?"

The generous offer was rewarded by a gasp from Louisa. "And permission for Amos to build me a fire—if that's all right with you, Mr. Burnside," Maggie added, her chin a stubborn line.

Rafe sent her steely look, but she noticed that he didn't say, either way. A hundred dollars was a lot of money and they all knew it.

"Cabin three will do, Amos," Louisa said quickly. "Last I checked, there was still a bit of wood in the fireplace."

Amos was thrilled to be allowed. "Will do!" he said, saluting smartly as he tugged his hat over his golden fall of hair.

"Thank you, Amos," Maggie said quietly, and was rewarded by his big, red blush. "I'll bring my van around as soon as I pay Mrs. Haymaker."

His slender shoulders hunched against the rain, Amos grabbed the cabin key from the wall board hook and dashed out the door, a damp chill sweeping the room as he left. The crisis, real or imagined, was over. "Thank you for allowing me to stay, Mrs. Haymaker. I'll just make you out that check and be on my way. I'm pretty tired."

Rafe must have understood something of Maggie's misery because, even though he looked as if he'd swallowed a lemon, he *did* back off. "I'll go help the boy," he muttered.

Louisa, too, seemed relieved. "Look here, Rafe. The little miss is a godsend. Her being a doctor means you won't have to drive me over to Bloomville next week, to see that podiatrist fellow—if she would look at my feet, that is."

"I never complained," Rafe said tersely, as he headed for the door.

"I know that, Rafe. You're as good as gold about that sort of thing. But it *would* be one less chore for you."

"I would be happy to examine your feet, Mrs. Haymaker," Maggie said quickly as she followed Rafe, "just as soon as I'm on my own." Then, no longer able to hide her exhaustion, Maggie bid Louisa good night. Standing outside, sheltered by the tiny porch, they both hesitated, neither anxious to step out into the storm. Every gust of wind sent a heavy spray of cold rain across their cheeks.

"I guess we had better make a dash for it, before we really get wet."

"*Really get wet?* What do you call this?"

The flickering yellow porch light barely lit the way, the relentless rain blurred the path, but Maggie could see Rafe clear as day. They were so close his breath was a warm whisper, and all the rain streaming down her body could not cool the heat suddenly coursing through her veins. Standing in the dark, wet wood of a misbegotten town, she watched his dark eyes narrow. It was there in his look, his reluctant gaze on her mouth, his slight, but unmistakable interest. She could almost see his own surprise, and his dismay, before he turned on his heel and hurried into the night.

Shaking sense into herself, Maggie tried to calm her beating heart. When she could breathe again, she made a mad dash for her van, turned on the ignition and blasted the heat high until some warmth crept back into her body. When she could wriggle her toes, she drove around back, to the line of cabins hardly visible. Thankfully, one reflected light. Ignoring her headache, she pulled a heavy valise from the back of the vehicle but it was so heavy, and she was so weak, she could hardly lift it. Frustrated, she left it where it fell and headed for the cabin, her sneakers making squishy, wet sounds that made her regret her rubber boots, buried somewhere in the back of the van. Next to the cold pills, she told herself ruefully.

The path she followed was short, but led directly to her cabin. And no matter what that grumpy man said, Louisa Haymaker *was* interested in clients, if that scraggly pot of flowers standing by the door was any indication. The poor woman had obviously tried to bring some color to the otherwise dreary establishment.

Swinging wide the cabin door, Maggie hurried into the cabin. It was a shabby room that had seen better days, but she hadn't been expecting much. The bed was covered with a worn chenille spread, the curtains dusty, the furniture stained. Across the room, kneeling by the fireplace, Amos was trying valiantly to light the smokiest fire she had ever seen. Coughing loudly, she hoped the sound would herald an end to his struggle. Amos scrambled to his feet, embarrassed, but full of pluck.

"Don't you worry, miss, I'll have this fire lit in a jiffy," he promised as he worked some kindling into a fresh bundle.

"Maybe you want to use some paper, too, Amos. Those sticks look a bit moldy. What do you think?"

"Rafe says that using paper to start a fire is cheating."

"Your father has a lot of opinions," Maggie said neutrally.

"Oh, yes, ma'am. He's the smartest man in Primrose. Everyone says so."

"Do tell," Maggie murmured as she discovered the heating unit that stood beneath the window. Raising the metal lid that covered the controls, she flipped the switch that indicated *heat* and was rewarded with a short, loud bang, a few clickety clacks, and finally, a low hum. Holding her hand over the feeble jet of air, she actually felt something resembling warmth. Turning to Amos, she sent him a rascally smile. "*That's* cheating, Amos, and you may tell your father I said so!"

"You may tell him so yourself," she heard a deep voice grumble.

Maggie turned to find Rafe Burnside looming in the doorway, holding the valise she had abandoned. He probably didn't even know he was looming, but there could be no other word, he was such a big man. A big, grim man.

"I found your bag sitting in a mud puddle."

Maggie watched as he strode into the cabin, casting a long shadow that seemed to block out the cheap plastic furniture, the dingy yellow wallpaper, the frayed blue carpet. His lanky body stood out in stark relief, and when he brushed past, to set her muddy valise near the bed, he carried the scent of the woodlands. Unnerved by the impact he had on her, Maggie strove for a semblance of normality, digging for it in the bottom of her bag.

"Here, Amos, please let me give you something for all your help," she said pulling out her wallet. "I don't know what I would have done without your help."

His eyes angry slits, Rafe froze her with a curt warning. "Amos doesn't need your money, Doctor Tremont. Whatever the boy does, he does out of kindness."

Embarrassed, Maggie quickly backed off. "I didn't mean to insult anyone. I just thought—"

Whatever she was going to say didn't matter because Rafe was gone, out the door before she could finish her sentence. Amos scrambled to his feet to follow his dad, but not before he left with one last sunny smile. "Good night, Doctor Tremont."

"Thank you, Amos. Good night. It was so nice to meet you."

Then Amos was gone, too, following hard on his father's footsteps. Maggie watched from the cabin door as they climbed in their truck, listened as Rafe turned on the ignition and drove away, until the only thing visible was the distant flicker of red taillights, a blur in the pouring rain.

Leaning against the doorjamb, Maggie took a moment to catch her breath. *What on earth had just happened?* What made her heart beat so fast? Surely not the sight of a grown man in desperate need of a shave? Suddenly her whole world was askew, hostage to new emotions. Worrying that her nose wasn't quite as chapped! Wondering whether her bedraggled state was that off-putting. Wondering when she was going to see that dreadful man again because, no matter what he thought of her, *she* found herself suddenly consumed with thoughts of a total stranger!

Primrose. The town that time forgot.

Standing in the middle of a drafty, moldy cabin, shaking her damp curls free of their confining clip, Maggie had a hunch that whoever named the town had been generous. To be named after a flower was unlooked for charity whose bounty had been repaid

a long time ago. Certainly there was nothing cha-
ritable in the angry scowl of a bitter man.

When Maggie woke early next morning, the
room heater had warmed and dried the air, but the
rain outside was still an unpleasant patter that didn't
know it was July. It was the drippy faucet her nose
had become, not to mention her raging headache,
and aches and pains, that said there was no way she
was leaving her bed. The doctor who cured everyone
else had finally succumbed to her patients' ailments.
One too many coughing, wheezy patient had finally
done her in. Ignoring her own health had been a big
mistake, she could see that now. What else could you
say when you were stuck in the middle of nowhere
with a respiratory-tract infection and not a cup of tea
in sight? Too drained to even use the bathroom, she
burrowed back beneath the warm covers, clutching
a handful of soggy tissue to her nose. At some point,
a glass was pressed to her lips and she obeyed the
gruff voice commanding her to drink. Tea, sweet-
ened with honey, a balm to her burning throat. But
no matter how much the gruff voice ordered, she
could not manage more than a few sips. Her strength
was negligible and she sank back into a deep sleep,
unaware of the calloused hand that gently brushed
her damp hair from her cheek. She figured she had
dreamed it, had imagined, too, the scent of pine that
floated on the air.

The only thing that roused her later that day was
Louisa Haymaker poking hard at her shoulder.

"Come on, Doctor Tremont, time to wake up. It's going on one o'clock, and I brought you a nice cup of chamomile tea and some aspirin."

Stirring reluctantly, Maggie pried open her swollen, watery eyes to find Louisa Haymaker's pendulous face hovering over hers. Spotting the tea cup sitting on the night table, she tried to rouse herself into a sitting position, but was unable to do so.

"Look, miss, you have to wash down these aspirin. When I didn't see you this morning, I figured you were probably feeling a bit poorly."

"I *am* feeling poorly!" Maggie croaked as she swallowed the aspirin Louisa had brought, sounding more like a frog every minute. "But weren't you here? I thought…"

"My, my, you *are* a sick little thing, aren't you?" Louisa declared grimly. "And *you* a doctor! Well, what am I to do?"

"You don't have to *do* anything," Maggie promised. "Just let me stay a few days and I'll be fine. It's only a cold."

Humph. "Doctor Tremont, I lived through three influenza epidemics. I think I know the flu when I see it."

The next time Maggie woke, it was to the sound of chirping birds and bright sunlight streaming through the window, lighting the room and warming her face as it dappled across the bed. She had no strength to move, but she *could* turn her head, even if it felt like a rock quarry. When she did, she was surprised to see Rafe Burnside staring at her from a nearby chair, his long legs sprawled awkwardly before him.

"It's about time you're up," he grumbled.

Groggy and headachy, Maggie didn't say anything, but, oh, for goodnes's sake, there went her heart thumping away again, at the very sight of him. What was it about this man that sent her into a tailspin? It was almost elemental, the way her body swung into high alert, even with a fever! Clearing her throat, she pretended not to be affected by his presence.

"What time is it?" she asked hoarsely.

"Near noon," he said as he rose to his feet. "Why do you want to know the time? It's not like you're going anywhere, is it?"

"Force of habit," Maggie said irritably. "What are *you* doing here?"

Rafe's mouth twitched. It had been a long time since someone sassed him and he found it amusing. "I was passing by and stopped to see how Louisa had survived the storm."

"How did she do?" she asked on a spate of coughing, forgetting that she had seen Louisa that very morning.

"A whole lot better than you," Rafe said, handing her a box of tissue. "She only suffered minor damage. Her storm door needs fixing, a few branches snapped, but beyond that, nothing major. I'll clear out the branches and see to the door when the weather clears."

"You take good care of her. Are you related?"

"No, but in Primrose we don't have to be related

to take care of each other. On the contrary, she sent *you* some tea," he said, his voice thickly ironic.

Embarrassed by her blunder, Maggie would have liked to ask Rafe to leave, but the way he fussed with the thermos, it seemed he wasn't going to until he served her tea. And though he might take her in dislike, Maggie noticed that the hands that helped her sit upright were careful to be gentle. Big, coarse hands, the sunburned hands of a farmer, thick at the wrist, sprinkled with black hair. Handsome hands, in their own way. She blushed when he caught her staring. Still, there was nothing in his manner that said he remembered the night before, or that anything had passed between them. And perhaps nothing had.

"What I wouldn't give for a shower," she murmured as he plumped up the pillows behind her.

"An idea that has merit," Rafe agreed as he handed her two aspirin, "but not an immediate prospect. Maybe tomorrow. Hot tea and aspirin, for now."

"Well, I appreciate your bringing it over."

"Louisa asked me to."

His terse retort made her blush. "Well, thanks anyway," she said, chagrined by his bad humor. "I think I can manage the rest."

"Really? Then I can leave? I'm off duty?" he asked as he poured her some tea.

But, weak as a kitten, the steaming cup shook so much in Maggie's hand that she was forced to accept Rafe's help. His know-it-all smile was so maddening that she found it hard to be gracious. She was annoyed, too, that he smelled so soapy clean and she felt so grungy. Hated that when he bent his head, his silky, black hair brushed her forehead, and was soft, and smelled of pine trees. But she hated *most* that when he held the cup of sweet, fragrant tea to her lips, his hand grazed her lips. She was glad that her falling hair hid the rush of heat that stained her cheeks.

"Where is Amos?" she asked between sips, deciding politeness was the best policy.

"The boy has his chores to do," Rafe said, matter-of-factly.

"Oh. Of course. Well, tell him I said hello."

Rafe said nothing.

"It looks like the rain's let up."

Rafe only nodded.

So much for small talk. Perhaps a show of interest in Primrose… "So, are you the town mayor, or something?" she asked lightly.

"Feeling better, are you?"

"What do you mean?"

"You just told a joke, I thought you might be perking up a bit."

"That wasn't a joke. I just thought—"

"Louisa insisted I check up on you, remember?"
Gee, thanks.

"I have to admit, though, she was right. You look pretty lousy."

Clutching the blankets to her chest, Maggie slid back down the pillow, wishing he were more…well, gallant… It was easier than telling herself she wished she looked like Greta Garbo in the final scene of *Camille*. She could not know the bewitching sight she made on her own, her auburn curls fanning the pillow, her large brown eyes a stark contrast to her pale, translucent skin.

"I guess I look too sick for you to throw me in my van and point toward the highway." No doubt he was wishing he had done just that, the way he was staring at her. The thought that he couldn't do so was oddly comforting.

"Something like... On the other hand, I wouldn't want to have you on my conscience."

As if you had one!

"Well, if there's nothing else you need," he said, suddenly busy with the thermos, "I guess I'll head back home and see what Amos is up to."

"If you gave me the number of a local restaurant, I could order in."

Caught off guard, Rafe surprised her with the hint of a smile. "We don't have restaurants here in Primrose!"

"No restaurants?" Maggie's face reflected her amazement. "Not one?"

"Not one! Not even fast food."

"What *do* you have in town?"

"We don't really *have* much of a town, Doctor Tremont. More like a loose confederation."

"A confederation of what?"

"*Of families*, Doctor Tremont. Families who take care of their own. We need help, we ask each other. It's worked pretty well, so far."

Chapter Three

Maggie slept off and on the next few days, gulping down the tea and aspirin Louisa periodically brought her. Nibbling on toast, she worked her way up to eating a boiled egg on the third day, the day her fever broke and she could feel her nasty bout with the flu start to break up. No one was more grateful than she when, waking that morning, she could stretch without setting off a time bomb in her head. A perfect opportunity to sneak in a long-overdue shower.

Planting her feet firmly on the cold parquet floor, she found she was steadier than she'd expected. On that positive note, she headed for the bathroom, stripped to the buff and stood beneath the shower, delighting in the blessedly hot stream of water that rained down on her clammy, sour skin. Shampooed and soaped, she left the shower ten minutes later, not wanting to test the capacity of Louisa's hot water tank. By the time she found a fresh nightgown and dried her hair, she was exhausted. Flicking back the blankets, she slid back into bed, asleep in moments. An hour later, turning on a stretch, she opened her eyes to find Rafe standing by the lone, small table, cradling a small covered pot.

"Do you always enter without knocking?" she asked, rubbing the sleep from her eyes.

"I knocked, but you didn't hear me, and this pot is pretty hot. Are you always so cranky when you wake up?"

Rummaging about in a cardboard box he had also brought, Rafe removed a bowl, some utensils, and a bag of bright red apples. "From my farm. I own an apple orchard. The Burnside Apple Orchard."

"You grow apples? Why, they're beautiful," Maggie admired.

"Fresh from the tree. They'll be crisp, maybe even a little tart, it's a bit early for apples."

"I prefer tart apples. And I appreciate your effort. *Really!* An apple a day, you know…"

"Yeah, well. It doesn't seem to work too well for you."

"Maybe that's because they weren't from your orchard."

Rafe turned away, but Maggie could tell he was pleased with her compliment. "So, I guess you're on the way to recovery, if those wet towels in the bathroom are any indication," he said, glancing at the damp brown ringlets that haloed her face.

Surprised that he noticed, Maggie said nothing. But his fleeting look reminded her that she was wearing only a thin nightgown. She was careful to bring the blankets with her, when she scooted up against the pillows.

"I feel like I just survived a ten-round bout with Mohammed Ali," she laughed, "but I'm definitely on the mend. Don't believe that pile of tissues," she warned when she saw him eye the overflowing wastebasket beside her bed. "I'm sneezing less. And if my appetite is any indication… Whatever you have in that pot, kind sir, set it right down here!" she commanded him. "I'm going to eat the whole thing!"

"It's only a Scotch broth. Last night's dinner. But it seemed the right thing to bring."

"Last night's dinner? Well, I'm not complaining. But what is a Scotch broth?" Maggie asked as she dipped her spoon in the bowl. "Not that I wouldn't eat whatever it was. It smells heavenly."

Rafe's shaggy brow rose. "You mean you actually *like* turtle soup?"

Seeing Maggie hesitate, Rafe sent her a lopsided grin. "You just said you'd eat anything,"

"Well, yesss… I suppose…"

"For Pete's sake, lady! A Scotch broth is a soup made from lamb and barley."

"I knew that!" Maggie said, ignoring his skeptical look as she tasted her first spoonful. "Wow, this is wonderful."

"I'll tell Amos you said so. It was really his idea to bring you some."

"But you were the chef?"

Walking to the window, Rafe said nothing, but Maggie was beginning to realize that Rafe Burnside didn't bother to answer the obvious. Studying his back, she ate quietly, but not as much as she'd thought she would. Her stomach refused to take in more than a few mouthfuls. Setting aside her bowl, she leaned back with a sigh.

"You know, that gorgeous sun… It would be nice to sit outside a while. Only a few minutes," she said quickly, when she saw him frown.

"I suppose," he shrugged. "If you managed to walk to the shower… It *is* July, after all. Your being a doctor, you *would* know what's best."

His irony not lost on her, Rafe set Maggie's valise on the bed and told her he'd wait outside. Minutes later Maggie joined him, wearing clean jeans and wrapped in a blue wool sweater. Settling in a worn Adirondack chair, she leaned back and sighed happily. "Hmm, just what the doctor ordered. *Sunshine*, the best medicine."

Almost, she could feel him frown. "Are you really a doctor?"

"Really and truly," she promised. "I don't know why everyone keeps asking me that."

"Maybe it's because you look so young," he said, staring thoughtfully at her red toenails as they peeked from beneath her sandals.

Maggie blushed. Compliments about her looks came rarely, and she was never sure how to accept them. And then, she wasn't even sure he *had* complimented her. His voice had *sounded* approving, but carried a gruff quality she could not account for.

Maggie had Rafe's approval, even if she didn't know it. The freckles dusting her pale cheeks, her pointy chin high, a smile on her pink lips, Maggie had no idea how appealing she looked. She had always disparaged her unruly brown curls, but watching them gleam in the sunlight, admiring their red and gold glints, Rafe thought she looked…nice. Not that he cared. He didn't care. It was just a thought.

"Where's Amos?" she asked, her face tilted to the warm sun.

"Busy."

"Oh, right. His chores. I forgot. But isn't it Sunday?"

"Cows don't know about Sunday." Rafe snorted. "Or Christmas, or the Fourth of July, for that matter. They just know they like to get milked."

"When does he have time to play, with all those chores to do?"

"When his chores are done. It's good for kids to have responsibilities. It's only two cows. When he's done, he's going canoeing with his friends."

"No canoe trips for you?" Maggie smiled.

"Not in years," Rafe said, his eyes flat and unreadable.

"Does that mean that you took time from your own chores to deliver that stew?"

"I can handle the extra load. I'll finish up my chores as soon as I leave here. What about you? Now that you're on the mend, don't you have a schedule to keep, somewhere to be?"

"Trying to get rid of me already, Mr. Burnside?" Maggie grinned. "Watch out you don't hurt my feelings."

"You were supposed to be here in April, so I thought maybe—"

"Mr. Burnside, you mistake the matter. If you are referring to the medical van, *I* wasn't supposed to be here, *or anywhere near here*, and furthermore, I have no idea what happened to the van, last April, as I've already explained to Louisa. But I swear," she said, plainly exasperated, "first thing tomorrow morning, I'm going to call the office and find out what's going on. I hope to be able to satisfy everyone concerned," she added pointedly.

"People have a right to health care," Rafe insisted. "We pay our taxes just like the folk in Bloomville— who just got a fancy, new hospital, by the way—so we have a right to expect the van to show up when it's supposed to. This isn't the kind of town where you can get on a bus and go see your doctor. *There is no doctor.* A town like Primrose—" Rafe hesitated "—a town like Primrose has special needs. I just want to see them met. Like a visit from the van, now and then. We're not asking for a hospital, or even a clinic. A thing like that brings complications."

"Complications?"

"Bureaucracy…government officials asking

dumb questions…five tons of paperwork to fill out just to remove a splinter…that sort of thing. But a visit from the van, time to time, that would be nice. Anything really serious, we go to Bloomville."

Surprised by Rafe's passionate outburst, Maggie didn't know what to say. "Mr. Burnside, when I call the department, maybe I can get them to juggle my schedule and let me stay."

"They should, if they know what's fair," Rafe said quietly.

"I can only try," she warned.

"Don't worry, I won't count on it." Rafe shrugged impatiently as he Rose to his feet. "Well, seeing as how you are finally able to move about, I don't think you'll be needing me anymore. Louisa says to tell you she'll provide you with your meals until you leave. Another day or so, and you'll feel your old self again."

"Gee, thanks," she murmured. "Just what I want, to feel like, *my old self.*"

And *almost,* Maggie thought, astonished by the sight, *almost* Rafe's lips twitched. But no, that couldn't be. She might not know Rafe Burnside very long, but intuition told her that laughing was alien to the man.

Maggie watched as Rafe headed for his truck, a mud-splattered red Ford that had been new in another lifetime. His long denim-clad legs made short work of the muddy path, his dusty boots were a sure step on the rough road. Truly, he *was* a son of the soil. A lonely man doing a lonely job, she mused as she watched him drive away, his battered gray hat shielding his eyes. All those hours alone, clearing land, seeding, harvesting his apples, threshing (whatever *that* was), milking cows, cleaning out the barn... What did he think about, perched high on his tractor day after day, hour after hour, row after row? How many times had he conquered the world in his imagination? Or did he only think about the price of seed, whether his son was going to need a new pair of boots the coming winter? Or perhaps he had *no* imagination; maybe he just emptied his mind and let his thoughts float on the wind. Row after row, endlessly, every season. It made her wonder if *she* could do it. It made her wonder *why* he did.

Dozing in the late afternoon sun, Maggie had the strangest dream about a tall, suntanned man, cornstalks, and endless fields of soft, green clover tickling her bare feet. She was almost disappointed when Louisa woke her, tapping on her shoulder in the twilight of the evening. "Wake up, Miss Tremont. I thought you might want to join me for dinner. Nothing fancy, but I didn't think you'd turn down a hot meal."

Her offer was a welcome invitation to Maggie's growling stomach. "You're right, Louisa, I wouldn't. Rafe Burnside mentioned you had offered to feed me."

Louisa was surprised. "Rafe was here?"

"That he was," Maggie said as she stretched herself awake. "Earlier this afternoon."

"Strange. I wasn't expecting him."

"He brought me some Scotch broth."

"How interesting," Louisa murmured.

"It was delicious! Unfortunately, I couldn't eat too much, but not for want of trying. My stomach just wasn't ready."

Following the old woman's lumbering steps down the path, Maggie listened to Louisa's cane tapping on the uneven slate pavement. Since the rain had stopped, the path had become less muddy, but it was still a slippery slope. She wondered how safe it was for Louisa to live alone but didn't like to pry. She had made enough demands on the poor lady.

Louisa's home turned out to be a small apartment situated above the store. Following the old woman up a rickety flight of stairs, Maggie was welcomed into a living room filled with a lifetime of memories and mementoes.

"How nice," she said, taking a close look at the fading pictures on the wall.

"If I had a housekeeper, now *that* would be nice," Louisa chuckled as she set a pitcher of iced tea on the kitchen table. Set for two with pretty, speckled blue dinner plates, Louisa apparently hadn't expected a refusal. The tumblers were old jelly jars, and the forks and knives had long since lost their sheen, but the tablecloth was snow white. And whatever Louisa was cooking smelled terrific.

"Beef stew," she announced, as she placed a hot pot on a trivet in the center of the table.

Maggie was thrilled. "That smells amazing! It's been a hundred years since I had a home-cooked meal, and now, two in one day, I feel spoiled. Although I have to warn you, my stomach is not up to par."

"Eat what you can. I won't take offense."

"Good. Then I'll start with that terrific-looking bread," Maggie said, reaching for a thick slice. "Back home, I eat mostly cafeteria food. I spend a lot of time at the hospital," she explained when she saw Louisa's questioning look. "Boston Mercy Hospital. That's where my office is. I have a small private practice, too."

"So, you run around a lot. No family?"

"No family," Maggie admitted.

"It sounds lonely," Louisa observed.

Maggie was startled. Sometimes it was, but how could Louisa know? Disconcerted, her thoughts wandered as she buttered her bread. It was true. Although she had not put it into so many words, loneliness *was* at the core of her dissatisfaction, many months, now. It had begun to manifest when she allowed herself to be talked into mountain climbing—when she knew darned well she *hated* hiking! It had been the reason she had joined a gym, wondering if she needed more exercise. It was the reason she had joined a book club, thinking that perhaps she needed the intellectual stimulation. She knew she needed *something*, she just didn't know what, was only sure of a restlessness come upon her, the last year or so.

"Is this bread homemade?" she asked, wanting to escape her somber thoughts.

"Sourdough," Louisa said, unaware of the nerve she had hit. "My mother taught me how to bake bread. I've been doing it longer than I care to remember."

"Well, she did a good job," Maggie approved. "This is heavenly. I take it you were born here in Primrose?"

"Most folk hereabouts were."

"Rafe and Amos, too?"

Louisa nodded.

"And Amos' mother?"

"*That one*," Louisa huffed. "Long gone, is Mrs. Rose Burnside. She left soon after Amos was born, seven years ago. Stayed around long enough to wean her baby, then, *whoosh*, disappeared into the night."

Maggie was shocked. "She left her baby? Where did she go?"

Louisa shrugged her massive shoulders. "Don't ask me. No one knows."

"Not even Rafe?"

"If he does, he isn't saying. So many questions…" Louisa tsked.

"Oh, come on, Louisa," Maggie protested. "I stumble into a town that hasn't had a visitor in months—*your words*—somehow, I feel compelled to ask questions."

"I suppose, but Rafe would hate knowing we were talking about him. Not that there's all that much to tell. He came in from the fields one day looking for his dinner and found a note instead, Rose gone, and all his savings, too. A year later, he got a big, brown envelope from some fancy law office. Divorce papers. He never heard from Rose again."

"But that's so sad."

"Abandoning your baby is sad, too."

"I suppose," Maggie agreed slowly. "But—"

"No *buts* about it, dearie. To tell the truth, though, there were signs, Rafe just didn't want to see them. You ever hear the phrase *a fool for love?* Well, that was Rafe Burnside. See, Rose wasn't like everyone else. She was beautiful, *movie-star beautiful*, and didn't she know it. Long blond hair and big, blue eyes will do it every time. Always hounding the postman to deliver her those movie star magazines from Bloomville. Then she'd spend all her time reading them, cover to cover, copying the hairstyles, doing her nails—and not much else! Not that having clean nails is a bad thing." Louisa laughed as she sliced them more bread. "But it was suspicious-like, you know? Only, Rafe couldn't see it. And another thing. Of course, it's only *my* opinion," she said low, even though there was no one else to hear, "but *I* think she married Rafe for his money! Think what you will, child, but money is mighty important to those that don't have. Poor as church mice, her family was. And Rafe had just finished building himself a sweet log cabin up in the hills. Real handsome too, he was, in his younger days. A big, strapping lad… Like my Jack," she sighed, but quickly shook away the past. "Anyway, ten months after they got hitched she had that baby, but she was gone soon after Amos was born. I guess that log cabin wasn't to her liking."

Poor Rafe. Poor Rose. Poor kids, both of them.

Married so young... Then, suddenly, a baby on the way...

Rafe... Rose... Amos... Three shattered lives. Part of the fabric of a town that wasn't even on a map.

"So, Louisa, what do you think?" The words popped out of Maggie's mouth before she could stop them, as she stood at the kitchen sink a few days later, soaping up the breakfast dishes. She did not want to give the old woman extra work if she could help it.

Having called her office, Maggie now awaited their decision whether she should remain in Primrose and provide the medical care the town had missed. But beyond that, no matter what her office decided, she decided to spend another few days in Primrose. To recuperate, she told Louise. To catch up on her sleep, finish the murder mystery buried somewhere in her van. It might have had to do, too, with the long walks she'd been taking around the beautiful countryside. Perhaps, too, the simple pleasure she found having breakfast in the early morning sun. But suddenly, and she could not explain it even to herself, she was in no hurry to return to Boston. So, she watched as Louisa toddled around her kitchen, wondering if she could read the answer in the old woman's stooped shoulders. Maggie had a vague feeling that the opportunity to act the mother hen might appeal to the elderly woman, that and the fact that the old woman was starved for company. She waited quietly as the old woman mulled things over, watched as Louisa wiped down the kitchen table and put away the salt shaker.

"I suppose it would be okay," Louisa began slowly.

Having learned a little about Louisa, Maggie knew to wait quietly as the old woman chose her words. Maggie detected a note of shyness in her voice. "I mean, why own a motel, if you don't want guests?"

A good question. Maggie had wondered the very same thing herself.

"A paying guest at that," Louisa observed. "I've had some that scooted away in the middle of the night," she explained. "But I can tell you're not the type."

Maggie shook her head. "Not the type, no," she promised as they settled the matter.

Two more days' rest and Maggie was her old self again. Her nose still betrayed the occasional sniffle, and her cough would probably linger for another week or so, but her energy was back, full throttle. And she had good news to impart. Her office had agreed she should remain in Primrose a few weeks and offer the town the medical care they had missed the previous spring.

"The head office was mortified when I spoke to them, and more than willing to rectify the error."

"And so they should," Louisa sniffed. "I'm glad

they had the decency to fess up. And I'm glad it's *you* who'll be doing the doctoring."

"I'm glad you're glad." Maggie grinned over a cup of chamomile tea she had brewed in Louisa's tiny kitchen. Having now shared a number of meals there, Maggie had grown comfortable moving about, and Louisa had given her free rein.

"Look, Maggie, I'm an old woman. I've lived in this town all my life. I don't *know* anything else, except that I'd like to know that Primrose will survive me. Is that so wrong?"

"Of course not," Maggie protested. "But you needn't talk like that. It was just a fluke that they missed the last medical rotation here."

"It's more than that. In a nutshell, we're too isolated," Louisa said promptly. "We always have been. It's okay to be a one-horse town, it preserves your heritage, and all—*I know that*—but isolation has its price, and the price for Primrose has been its decline. Plain and simple, we're sinking into poverty. Maybe once it was okay to farm *only,* but not any longer. The town is dying, and that's a fact."

According to the old woman, and she admitted that her memory might be faulty, quite a few babies had been born last spring. Well, they ought to be vaccinated, but they hadn't yet been. Although many townspeople came to town when the medical van came by, many did not. There were four, possibly five babies somewhere up in the mountains that needed their shots. Finding them would be difficult, too. But it wasn't *only* a matter of babies and vaccines; they were *all* in need of better health care. Her swollen legs were a prime example.

And there were countless other things, Louisa sighed.

Their lone school teacher was looking very peaky of late. Or maybe she was just getting old. After all, Ella *was* turning seventy-one next month.

The main road was in dire need of paving. So, even if Maggie wanted to stay and help, the roads were difficult to travel.

"We have to do something, pull things together somehow, plan for the next generation. I was thinking that maybe, while you were doing the clinic you could take some sort of survey, get some idea of what everyone's thinking."

"Louisa, why would the townsfolk talk to *me?* They don't know me, much less trust me, and after what happened with the van in April, I doubt if anyone here is inclined to confide in me."

Louisa looked at her blandly. "True," she said slowly, then brightened with a new thought. "But they'd talk to Rafe Burnside! They'd talk to *him!*"

"But you would have to get Rafe to help me, and from things he said, I would be surprised if he had any spare time."

"Never mind that. He'd do it, if I asked him, and it's only for a few days. If we gave him some sort of schedule I'm sure he could work around it. People have enormous respect for Rafe. They would definitely talk to him. Besides, some people won't know the van is here, so you're going to have to do some traveling to the outlying farms, and he could help you do that. Yes, getting Rafe to help you would be an excellent start."

Stifling a sigh, Rafe leaned back in his chair and closed his eyes. "Louisa's just feeling her age."

Intent on persuading Rafe, Maggie had cornered him the very next day, when he stopped for gas, winning him over with a glass of Louisa's home-made lemonade.

"Here, have another glass. She left me a whole pitcher, insisted it was a curative. She said in her day a *real doctor* would have prescribed a mustard plaster for a cold. A real doctor, indeed!" Maggie laughed, shading her eyes against the July sun that beat down as they sat outside Maggie's cabin. "Louisa's lemonade is so tart it could probably kill every germ in your body, *including* your white blood cells! As *a real doctor*, I know this for a fact!"

Watching Rafe's long fingers hug the frosty glass, Maggie marveled at her ability to make small talk. It had been a few days since she'd last seen him, and she hadn't known him much longer than that, but he did something to her insides that she couldn't explain. Watching him drink the tart lemonade in two long draughts, his firm jaw working, his Adam's apple bobbing… Babbling was the least of her problems. Lit by the sun, his carved, granite face seemed to take on a softer contour. His body in repose made a compelling argument for outdoor work. She wondered what time he started his day, and was sorry to bring him grief, since it was evident he did not want to hear what she was going to say.

"Rafe, yesterday, over breakfast, Louisa confided in me some of the things that are going on in Primrose."

Rafe handed Maggie the empty tumbler with a quizzical look.

"Sometimes it's easier to talk to a stranger," she explained. "She's very concerned and insists that the town has some big issues to deal with."

Rafe drew his hat over his eyes. Another do-gooder lands her angel wings in town. His disgust knew no bounds, even if he felt the faint tug of attraction for Maggie. Sure she was cute, cuter than most, but she was still only after one thing, to stir up the pot, make herself feel good, leave as soon as the hot water ran out. These government people had no staying power. Not many people did, he reminded himself grimly. Why then, should he put himself out? Pretty red toenails didn't mean squat, where he came from. Of course, if she wanted some action… Rafe laughed to himself, about himself. *Damned ugly old farmer, go look in a mirror. What would she want with you?* So he sighed for what could have been, and ignored Maggie's pretty toes.

"Like I said, Louisa's just feeling her age. She and I already had this conversation, when she called my house, last night. I told her straight out that I didn't have time. Anyway, she worries too much."

But Maggie would not be so easily dismissed. "Listen, cowboy, it's not fair to brush Louisa off that way. She has legitimate concerns about

Primrose. Oh, and just so you know, I got a call, too, early this morning. My office is letting me stay awhile and make amends to the town."

"A generous offer, considering you *are* a doctor."

"For your information, I do not run the program!" she snapped. "Someone else determines the schedule, and we have a very small staff that covers six states. Like I said, I'm going to stay a week or two, to help out, but I refuse to play the blame game. Louisa, on the other hand, was talking about the town's *survival*. She has a shopping list, too, a big one. New roads, a new schoolhouse, and a new teacher to put it to use. But mostly she talked about how the town was on the brink of ruin. She's very concerned about that, and wants to find ways to raise revenue. She has some good ideas, too."

"And you've been here how long?" Rafe drawled, lifting his hat to send her a searching look. "Three days?"

"I know." Maggie blushed. "I sound like a know-it-all, but I was only her sounding board. Still, she's right to be concerned. Nothing lasts forever. Things change…people… Towns do, too."

"Yeah, and people come and go, too."

Maggie winced at the bitterness she heard in Rafe's voice, sighed too, for the discouraging message he sent. She didn't blame him for not trusting her, a perfect stranger charging into his life, but on the other hand, Louisa had chosen her, not the other way around. She was determined not to be cowed. "Look, Rafe, could we please keep this simple? Louisa thinks there were about half a dozen babies born last winter and they haven't had their shots. She knows who they are, but she says I need someone to take me around, that they are not going to necessarily know I'm here, and that finding their homes could take *me* forever."

"You like children?" It was a statement more than a question.

"Yes, I do, as a matter of fact. Very much," she admitted.

"But you have none of your own? No Prince Charming ever swept you off your feet?"

"Prince Charming? Are you serious? Does he actually exist?"

"No more than Cinderella, I guess."

Maggie laughed. "Well, the answer is, no, I never married. I don't go to many balls in my line of work."

"Don't know the last one I was at either, now that I think about it."

"It wouldn't have mattered," Maggie said. "I can't have children. A massive infection saw to that a long time ago."

"Oh." Rafe frowned. "Well, that's too bad."

"It happens." Maggie shrugged, a distant look in her eyes. "It was a long time ago. I've come to terms with it. Although I *would* have liked to have gone to a ball. Things work out how they will." She shrugged.

"That they do," Rafe agreed quietly.

They sat for a minute or so until Rafe rose to leave.

"So, what about Louisa's idea that you could help introduce me around?"

"You *do* know I have a farm to run, don't you?"

"If we did it, now, before the harvest…"

Rafe smiled. "And what would you know about *the harvest?*"

"I know it's not in July." Maggie grinned, refusing to be goaded.

"Oh, really? Ever hear about *putting up the hay*, little girl?"

Little girl? Maggie blushed. So what if Rafe was six feet plus? At five feet eight, no one had ever called *her* little! And it was totally sexist, although she had a hunch Rafe wouldn't have cared, if she told him. So then, what was there about it she *liked?* Because she was feeling mighty pleased with the world, at just that moment.

"Okay, Mr. Burnside, so what I don't know about farming could fill a book, but I'm not quite as ignorant as you would like to think. I was born and raised in a mill town set in the middle of dairy country. Isn't that near enough to farmland?"

"And that makes you know *something* about *something?*"

"*Something,* anyway." Maggie grinned. "Look, Rafe, how about we cut a deal? You help me get the neighborhood inoculated and I'll help you on the farm. I know it's too early to pick apples but maybe I could mow the lawn, weed or hay? Whatever."

Rafe looked down at her hands. "Those pretty pink nails are going to take quite a beating."

Maggie spread her hands wide. "You think?"

"I know!"

"Gloves?"

"They'll help *some*."

Maggie shrugged. She'd take her chances.

Chapter Four

After a short discussion with Louisa as to which families Maggie should visit, Maggie and Rafe made arrangements to meet the next morning. Rafe figured the whole job wouldn't take more than a couple of days. Moreover, he insisted they use his truck, arguing that Maggie's van would never survive the back roads.

"It always has before," Maggie argued, but Rafe would not be moved.

"I have no intention of changing a tire on a narrow, rock-strewn road just because you want to be stubborn."

"Excuse me?"

Maggie almost stomped her foot, but Rafe had

already walked away. So they spent the first half of the next morning sorting through her equipment, transferring her most essential supplies to his pickup.

And through it all, Amos sat in the middle of the truck cab, a wide grin on his face. Having learned of their plans the night before, he had campaigned hard not to be left out of the adventure. He had even awakened extra early—*while it was still dark out*, he told Maggie proudly—to do his chores before they left. Secretly, Maggie was glad the boy was there. Amos was so cheerful, he was a pleasure to have around.

If Rafe's dour face was any indication, he didn't share his son's enthusiasm. He had even made a fuss about the lunch basket Louisa had prepared for them. How, Maggie wanted to know, could he possibly refuse an old woman's kindness? What could he possibly have against eating lunch, especially when he had a growing boy to feed, she argued, playfully mussing Amos' yellow hair. Annoyed, Rafe had climbed into the driver's seat, his mouth grim and taut. Unperturbed, Maggie winked at Amos and climbed into the passenger seat.

Truthfully, Rafe was not annoyed. Actually, he was pretty pleased, Maggie just didn't know how to read him. He would have counted himself a fool not to realize his good fortune being tied—metaphorically speaking, of course—to an interesting woman like Maggie. Her energy, her smile and her kindness charmed the socks off Rafe. Not that he would admit to it. Which is why he wore the most somber face he could, pretended not to listen to her funny stories, and refused to share in the joke fest she and Amos got up, as they drove up the mountain. Never taking his eyes from the road, not missing a word she said, the chain wrapped around his heart began to loosen with every mile they drove.

And why not? When, in the last seven years, he asked himself, had he permitted himself the liberty to enjoy the company of a woman? Primrose was such an open book that if he even looked at another woman, the town was ready to send out wedding invitations. But this errand of Louisa's answered quite well for his purpose: he got to spend time with a woman he found very attractive *without having to declare any intentions.* And if anyone asked, he wouldn't have owned to any. He simply wanted to enjoy the company of a woman, take pleasure in the sound of feminine laughter.

Maggie hated to admit it, but Rafe had been right, the White Mountains were rugged, and the road made for an uncomfortable trip where it was not paved. But New Hampshire was lovely, no question. She had traveled much of New England, but something about the tiny state struck a chord. The forest they drove through was an exquisite blue-green canopy of pungent pines, and lush oaks and maples, their woody scent a delight to a girl whose life had been charted by the concrete sidewalks of a dull and austere mill town. Maggie was enchanted by the peaceable, quiet beauty of the lush trees and the soothing sound of birds chirping in the early-morning heat of July.

And Rafe, navigating roads he must have driven half a million times, his silhouette stern and uncompromising, his black hair fluttering across his brow in the warm morning breeze, well, she thought he was beautiful, too. Even the way he frowned at the road was attractive. Setting aside her worries, she was glad that he was there, and was thankful for his offer to drive her.

Offer? Maggie caught herself with a wry smile. *Wrong word, there, lady.* Even now, she was unsure why Rafe had agreed to accompany her. But she was grateful. His long fingers curved lightly on the steering wheel were somehow reassuring.

The first stop they made was at the Congreve farm. The Congreves were a family of seven—Frank and Fannie, and their five brawny, brawling boys. The homestead consisted of a rambling log cabin of irregular shape, no doubt because it had seen many additions, and need dictated style. Two sturdy sheds, a neatly fenced field and patches of grass begging for sunlight survived between small puddles of brackish water and mud. Parked beneath a huge tree was a rusty tractor that two young boys were pretending to drive, and which a third little boy was begging to join. A set of twins watched from a playpen set in the shade of the cabin porch.

As children, Rafe and Frank had idled away many an afternoon, fishing, hanging out and stealing fruit from their neighbor's trees. Amos did the same now, with Frank's boys. Except for the part about the stealing fruit, of course. Now that Rafe owned an apple orchard, he didn't view things in quite the same way. And neither did Amos, he said, glancing at his son. But the way Amos smiled, Maggie wasn't too sure about that.

She was surely charmed by the boisterous Congreve clan, though. When the older boys saw the Burnside truck, they slid down the tractor and ran to greet their visitors, shrieking and waving their arms. When Maggie saw Rafe deliver up a small brown bag, she understood why. She should have thought to bring candy. *She* would remember, next time.

"Hey, boys," Rafe said, returning their waves as he scooped up the youngest Congreve. "Is your mother about?"

"Yes, sir, she's in the house, cooking."

Something she probably does about fifteen hours a day, Maggie guessed.

"Good. I've brought this lady to meet your family. This is Maggie Tremont. *Doctor* Maggie Tremont. Dr. Tremont, meet the Congreve men."

The boys were polite, they cordially returned her greeting, but their eyes never left the brown bag dangling from Rafe's hand. As Rafe said their names, Fannie Congreve came striding across the front lawn, wiping her hands on a kitchen towel.

"Rafe! I thought I heard something! How good to see you," Fannie said, giving him a hug.

"Fannie," Rafe returned her greeting as he balanced the small child in his arms.

"And Amos! It looks like you've grown some, since I last saw you," she said, smothering the small boy in an embrace.

"But, Mrs. Congreve, I saw you on Sunday, don't you remember?" Amos protested.

"Then it must be something in the water." Fannie laughed.

Everything about Fannie Congreve was thin, not only her face but her long, lean body; but her smile was wide, her brown eyes shining happily as she turned to Maggie and waited politely for Rafe to introduce her to his friend.

"Hi, I'm Maggie Tremont," Maggie said, not waiting on Rafe.

"I'm Fannie Congreve." Fannie smiled back. "Glad to meet you, but not as glad as Maurice, it seems."

Maggie laughed as baby Maurice wriggled in Rafe's arms, stretching toward Maggie.

"I never saw him take to a stranger like that." Fannie smiled as Rafe handed Maurice to Maggie. "Must be a sign? What do you think, Rafe?"

Rafe shrugged. "I don't believe in that stuff. You know that."

"Rafe's always teasing me," Fannie explained to Maggie. "I believe in astrology and stuff, and read my horoscope every day. But it sure *seems* like a sign, the way Maurice has zeroed in on you. Kids are pretty sensitive."

Rafe didn't hesitate to play down the significance of Maggie's visit. "Yeah, but they're not magical, Fannie. Maggie is a doctor, a member of the Mobile

Clinic of New England that operates the van that missed us, last spring."

"That's not *entirely* correct," Maggie said, sending Rafe a sharp look. "I *am* a member of the mobile clinic, but *not* part of the team that missed Primrose. The head office has asked me to make up for the lost visit. I am guessing that there are a number of towns the van missed. They're going to let me know. Actually, Rafe's been kind enough to be *my* doctor the past few days. I stumbled into Primrose with the worst cold imaginable and he and Louisa Haymaker pitched in to nurse me back to life. Louisa has rented me a cabin at her motel and is cooking my meals, but Rafe offered to drive me around the area now that I'm feeling better, so that I could treat as many people as possible."

Fannie's look of disbelief was unmistakable.

"She sort of *insisted*," Rafe said vaguely. "And now that you two have been introduced, I think maybe I'll leave you girls to get to know one another. Hey, boys, want to show me where your da is working?"

"Rafe!"

"Come on, Fannie. You two are going to make girl talk, and I'm going to go crazy listening."

Rafe grinned as he motioned the giggling children to follow him. The two women watched as the children jumped on the bed of the pick-up and Rafe drove away.

"Isn't that just like that man!" she said to the dust he left behind.

"I wouldn't know, but from what I've seen... Yes." Maggie smiled. "That is just like Rafe!"

"Doctor Tremont—"

"Maggie, if you would."

Fannie smiled. "Maggie, then. I was just about to have some coffee. Why don't we share a cup out here on the porch? Being shut in the house can make for a very long day, especially on laundry day."

"I'll just bet," Maggie said. "And with twins, too, I can't imagine how you do it."

"Sending the boys off to school helps a lot! Whenever someone asks me if I'm in favor of a longer school year, I always say yes!" She chuckled as she headed indoors. "There are only so many snowmen a child can make."

"Mrs. Congreve—"

"It's Fannie, please. Why don't you hold on while I go get us some coffee? You can set Maurice back in his playpen. Zack, there, was giving him a hard time, which he often does, don't you, Zack?"

Fannie knelt to retrieve Zack's pretzel, then hurried into the house, returning moments later with two steaming mugs. "I took the liberty of adding milk, but I guessed at *no sugar*. I figured a doctor knew better."

"I do," Maggie said, glad of the coffee Fannie handed her.

"It's a minor miracle that Rafe brought you up here," Fannie told her as they got comfortable. "We don't really have any ongoing medical care, except when the van comes by, and when the van missed us... If you've seen Louisa's legs, you know what I mean. I'm pretty good at home cures, and what I don't know, someone else around here does, but we can't do shots and stuff. I don't mean to complain, we've been lucky, although I'm not sure Cyrus Halper would agree," she said thoughtfully as she cradled her mug. "He cut his foot pretty bad last year—right down to the bone—when he fell off his thresher. Rafe sewed him up until they could get him to Bloomville, and he did a pretty good job, too, but I have a hunch that Cyrus would have been glad to be put out."

"Put out? You mean with anesthesia?"

"Right, anesthesia." Fannie laughed. "They had to get him drunk just to bear the pain, which was the source of his problem in the first place."

"The pain?"

"The drinking!" Fannie explained with a short laugh. "But good came of it. Old Cyrus hasn't touched a drop since, and swears he never will."

"But how did Rafe know what to do?"

"Oh, Rafe's been doing that kind of stuff all his life. He delivered Amos when his wife went into early labor. Rafe knows *everything*," she said confidently. "He's a good man. A girl could do worse, not that whatshername thought so. Now, what was her name? *Risa? Rosa? Rose?* That was it, Rose! Left him the minute she could stand! Good riddance, as they say."

Watching Fannie as she took a minute to fuss with the twins, Maggie thought that if Rafe wanted a crown, unlike Caesar, he would have no trouble. For sure, he was king of *this* mountain, positively worshipped and adored, from everything she had heard. He was the beginning, the middle and the end for this community.

Poor Rose. It must have been hard to live with a legend.

Maggie was surprised to hear Fannie speak so frankly to a stranger, but in the next twenty minutes that they sat rocking on the porch, Fannie said nothing else revealing. The conversation wandered around many issues, but Rafe was no longer one of them, and Maggie was relieved. Whenever his name was mentioned, her antennae went up, and it made her feel like she was prying. It was much more pleasant to sit in the shade and listen to Fannie talk about her geraniums while the babies napped.

"Perhaps you would like me to examine the twins while the boys are gone?" she offered when the babies woke thirty minutes later. "I brought my medical bag, and it's quiet, now. It *is* sort of the aim of this trip, to make things a bit more convenient for those people who can't manage to get to town on such short notice. I can examine the older boys another day."

"You would do that?" Fannie asked.

"I would be happy to oblige."

"Then I would be happy to accept!"

Maggie followed Fannie inside with the twins and they settled in the kitchen, where Fannie spread a clean towel on the table. Aside from a few thousand toys strewn everywhere, the house was immaculate. Much to Maggie's surprise, Maurice and Zack took their examinations in good temper. The healthy babes were back in their playpen in no time, gnawing on sourdough pretzels.

"An hour's peace and someone to talk to! *This* is my idea of heaven." Fannie sighed as she leaned back in her rocker. "Frank bought me this rocker when I had the twins. Said it was the least he could do. I told him that condoms were the least he could do!"

Maggie laughed at Fannie's frankness. Five kids… But Fannie looked young.

"That's right. Five kids in *nine* years," Fannie said, reading Maggie's mind. "So, now you know what *I've* been doing the last ten years, tell me about yourself."

"There isn't much to tell. I've been a doctor all my life. It's the only thing I ever wanted to be. And no, there's no lost husband lingering in my background, no nasty wounding divorce. Remember that dreadful thunderstorm we had, three or four nights ago? Well, I was driving through when I lost my way. I pulled into Louisa's gas station with my gas signal light literally on empty. She agreed to put me up, but the truth is I had such a bad cold, she could hardly turn me away."

"Knowing Louisa, I'll bet she tried!" Fannie snickered.

Maggie nodded, smiling at the memory. "Yes, she did, but I was pretty sick. Now that I'm back on my feet, I want to make up for the missing van. Hopefully, it will be a word of mouth connection because I do have a fully equipped van parked down at Louisa's motel. I was working Massachusetts for a friend when I got lost. But it's kind of hard to let everyone know I'm here, so Louisa persuaded Rafe to take me around."

"A small battle, I'll bet."

"To be honest, Primrose is *not* living up to its name," Maggie smiled. "I'm still not sure why he agreed. It could be Louisa warning him that if I traveled up the mountain alone, I would probably never be heard from again. And from the look of the roads we took coming up here, I think that might be true."

As they relaxed, Fannie grew even more talkative, and Maggie took the opportunity to ask her what she thought of Primrose's future. It turned out that Fannie had a pet project she'd been teasing Frank with all winter: she wanted to start a farmer's market. In fact, she had already contacted the New Hampshire Department of Agriculture and done some research on their Web site.

Maggie was impressed. "Have you mentioned this to anyone else?"

"You bet! I've spoken to almost all the women in Primrose and they're all very interested."

"Do you have a plan?"

Fannie smiled faintly. "Maggie, I have lots of plans—and five kids. Putting it into action is the problem."

"What about starting up a committee to investigate?"

Fannie grinned. "How long did you say you were staying?"

They were still talking when Rafe and Frank and the Congreve boys pulled up, looking for their dinner. Frank Congreve was a taciturn man, obviously tired from his day's work, but very pleased to meet Maggie. Tired as he was, though, his pleasure in his family revitalized him. And his adoration of his wife, to whom he constantly deferred, was more than obvious. Fannie insisted that Rafe and Amos and Maggie share their evening meal, and Frank seconded the invitation, scolding Rafe when he tried to decline.

It was nothing fancy, Fannie warned as they all entered the house, just chicken and dumplings. Frank's favorite, but the meal Fannie set before them was a first-rate dinner that Maggie knew was guaranteed to put inches on her hips. She had second helpings of everything. The meal was a noisy affair, and even Rafe was unusually animated. Maggie could only account for it as a result of the warmth of the Congreves. But at seven o'clock, Rafe pushed back his chair, patted his belly and said that if they didn't leave now, they never would. Amos had no objection, his head was already drooping. With promises of future visits, they were soon driving back down the mountain.

"What a sweet family," Maggie said as Amos fell asleep on her shoulder. "It must be comforting to know someone your whole life."

"All our lives," Rafe said briefly.

"You're lucky. I don't know anyone that long."

"I don't think about people in those terms."

Maggie sent him a wry look. "No, men usually don't."

Chapter Five

Rafe picked up Maggie at her cabin the next day, as promised, although Amos was nowhere to be seen. "We got home so late, I let him sleep in, then dropped him off at a friend's this morning. He was invited to go fishing. A kid has to do kid things once in a while, especially when it's summer."

Maggie bit her lip to keep from smiling. If his dour face was any indication, he didn't seem to believe his own words, but who was she to argue? No doubt it was aggravation enough just taking her around. But when she gently settled a lunch basket in the back of the truck, she noticed he didn't object.

They spent the next few hours roaming the countryside, making house calls. The weatherman had promised an unusually hot summer, and it seemed he was going to live up to his prediction that day. Knowing how much gas cost, Maggie didn't dare ask Rafe to use the truck's air conditioner, but she accepted every glass of lemonade she was offered that afternoon.

Rafe was her ticket. With Rafe, she wasn't *let into people's homes, she was invited in,* and it made all the difference. Not only was she able to provide rudimentary medical care, but she did as Louisa asked, and broached the problems of Primrose. Louisa had been very excited when Maggie reported her findings the night before. And it turned out that she *had* known about the farmer's market.

"Fannie has been playing with that idea for a while, now, but I wasn't sure if she still wanted to do it. I'm glad to know she does."

"Rafe says we're going to see even more people tomorrow. Apparently, there's a cluster of families that live over on the south side of the mountain?"

"Oh, yes, I know where he's taking you, over past Cory Lake. Good. It will be interesting to hear if anyone else has any ideas how to get this town on its feet."

Traveling with Rafe, Maggie quickly learned that the problems of Primrose went beyond the need for good medical care. Everything went into the land, they told her, sometimes at the expense of good housing, adequate clothing and a decent diet. Schooling was a sometime thing. If the harvest dragged into late fall… They shrugged. The children were needed in the fields. Surely Doctor Tremont could understand that.

Of course Maggie understood. When she mentioned Fannie Congreve's idea of a farmer's market, they were all ears. Some of the people she met had heard of Fannie's plan. Most were excited at the idea of a market, partly because it was a plan they could be part of, and partly because they might even benefit financially. Pies, jellies and jams, candles, needlepoint—they were ready when Fannie was. Maggie thought that if Fannie wanted to start up the market tomorrow, she would be fairly well supplied.

What she did not understand was Rafe's irritation when they stopped for lunch beneath the cool shade of a tree on the bank of Cory Lake. Spreading a blanket on the grass, Maggie sat the lunch basket in the shade and walked down to the shoreline. In the distance loomed the White Mountains, but from where they stood, on the shore of Cory Lake, the mountains were doubly reflected on the glass of dark green water, and the only sound was the croaking of a lone frog. It was so hot, even the birds had sought shelter, and not a leaf quivered on the tall trees that skirted the shore.

"Pretty, isn't it?" Rafe said in his low, gravelly voice as he stood beside her.

"Very," Maggie said softly.

"When all else fails, we have the land. It's everything."

Maggie and Rafe stood together, married to the

canvas that Mother Nature had painted. When they grew hungry, they returned to the canopy of leaves that shaded their basket.

"How come you had to talk about all that stuff?" Rafe asked, as he watched her open the straw basket.

"All what *stuff?*" Maggie asked as she handed him a sandwich.

"Fannie's push for a farmer's market."

"Oh, that. That was Louisa's idea. She asked me to take an informal survey about how to improve Primrose. I didn't know anything about the farmer's market until Fannie mentioned it the other day. Why do you ask? Don't you think it's a good idea?"

"I wouldn't know, but it doesn't matter. It's not going to go anywhere, anyway."

"Why do you say that? You don't know that."

"I know that it would take a lot of organization, something this town doesn't know how to do."

"Then teach them."

"If it means having our mountains trampled by tourists, cleaning up the crap they leave behind, dousing their campfires, and having our roads destroyed even more than they are now, I am totally against it."

"Enough to fight it?" Maggie asked, curiously. "Even if they made accommodations?"

Rafe thought for a moment. "I don't trust many people."

Maggie wasn't surprised. "That's your choice, of course, but Frank and Fannie don't strike me as the type to push an idea that would hurt their community. It would take so little to get this town going again, Rafe, and surely you aren't against its revival? When you think about it, a farmer's market would suit Primrose admirably. The goods are already in place. It seemed to me that everyone we've spoken to so far has something to offer. It's almost a no brainer. Goodness, anyone can start one on the side of a road, and they do, so what's the big deal about doing it here?"

"Last year, when Fannie was talking up the market, I heard talk about using the town square. That's not exactly the side of the road."

"I didn't know that. Still… Well, I won't be here for the showdown, so I hope you'll steer them in the right direction."

"That's not the sort of thing I do."

"Oh, you just throw darts at their dreams?" Maggie asked, smiled faintly as she searched for the napkins.

Rafe bristled. "I protect them from themselves. And I protect the mountains."

"Well, I'm not all so sure about the way you're doing it, but like I said, I won't be here to argue. I do have to say, though, that Primrose is beautiful. It would definitely be a summer destination for vacationers. Just look at this lake, it's gorgeous. A few cabins around the periphery, a boat slip…"

"That's what I'm afraid of."

"Well, it's either that, or…"

Maggie hated to sound harsh but Rafe needed a serious dose of reality. Fannie Congreve seemed to have her wits about her, but if the rest of the town didn't mobilize with her, in a few years there wasn't going to be a town. The kids would grow up and leave, their inheritance the forsaken homes of their parents. She had seen it many times, as she drove through Massachusetts. *For Sale* signs jabbed into the lawns of hundreds of abandoned homes. New England was dotted with towns that died from a lack of goods, or services, or a combination of both, offering no good reason for the next generation to stay. Sometimes, it was the fault of the local box store, so eagerly invited only to suck the livelihood from a small town when the mom and pop stores could not compete. Perhaps it was the outsourcing of jobs, or new technology, built-in obsolescence. And as far as she was concerned, Primrose was one of those towns on its last legs. It didn't have to be. For every town that died, there was a town that re-invented itself. Taking a deep breath, she tried to poke Rafe into the future.

"I know you see me as an outsider, Rafe, but it seems to me that some hard choices have to be made here in Primrose. This town is in dire straits, and if you're not part of the plan, you're going to be part of the problem."

"You think so?"

"Yes, Rafe, I think so," Maggie said, as gently as she could. "You may not like my diagnosis, and you don't have to swallow my bitter pills, but you cannot escape your complaint."

Feeling that she had given Rafe enough to think

about, Maggie walked down to the water's edge and circled the lake until she found a secluded grassy embankment. Shucking her shorts and shirt, she took a hesitant step toward the shore, her eyes darting to the stand of trees where she had left Rafe. But when her toes touched the rim of the lake water, all thought fled. Heaven at her feet! Oh, how wonderfully cool! Inch by inch, she stepped into the lake, careful not to skid on the slippery rocks and pebbles. Dipping her fingers into the cool sweet pond, she splashed her chest, her neck, sprinkled her burning neck, until she took courage by the tail and sank beneath the gentle waves of the icy, spring-fed lake. Her eyes closed against the sun's brilliance, Maggie lost all sense of time as she floated in the sun. What was she thinking, to lead the crazy life she led, running across a dozen states ten months out of the year? She was about to turn forty. What would she find on the other side of that milestone? More of the same?

"Anyone seeing you would think you had never swam before."

Startled, Maggie turned herself upright, spluttering as Rafe surfaced, not two feet away. "Rafe Burnside, you completely snuck up on me!"

Smiling mischievously, Rafe found his footing in the waist deep water. "Don't worry, Doc, you're completely covered by water."

Feeling the cold water lap her shoulders, Maggie prayed he was right. He *was* a foot taller, so naturally he would show more skin, but she wasn't entirely sure.

"If I can see you, then you can see me!"

"Are you looking?" Rafe smiled, his eyes teasing.

Almost, Maggie could feel the power that coiled beneath Rafe's hard muscles as they flexed against the water's chill. She had to admit he was wonderful to look at. A bronzed god, massive and confident, his ruggedness profoundly attractive. *Not that she was tempted. No, indeed!*

But if he took one step closer… "Mr. Burnside, don't you *dare* come any closer!"

Her face burning with embarrassment, Maggie watched Rafe take another step, the lake rippling in a hundred watery circles, his eyes dark. He was so close she could almost feel the heat that radiated from his hard, naked body. Mesmerized, she followed the trail of water that dripped down his body, matting the pelt of black hair that covered his chest and pebbled his flat brow nipples. Like a deer in headlights, she froze.

Rafe's mouth curled in a knowing smile. "I'm not going to attack you," he said softly, "if that's what you're worried about." Lightly, he fingered a loose wet curl pasted to her cheek. "It's just that, the way you were thrashing about, I wasn't sure if you could swim."

"I…I know how to swim," Maggie stammered, shivering at his light touch.

"Oh. All right, then I don't have to worry."

"No…you don't have to worry."

"Good. Then I'll turn around, if you like."

"Yes…yes…I'd like it if you turned around!"

Maggie stammered, but she noticed he didn't move. Quite the opposite. His fingers leaving a wet trail down her temple, he captured her chin and raised her face to his. *Omygodhewasgoingtokissher.* Maggie could hardly breathe.

But he didn't.

"I only peeked a little," he whispered as he swam away, his laughter floating on the cool current.

Disappointed and confused, Maggie floated away on daydreams better left unexamined, until she felt a chill seep into her bones. Reluctantly, she returned to dry land, gathered up her clothes and hurried into the woods to dress. Returning to the picnic blanket, she found Rafe lying in the shade, chewing on a blade of grass.

"Where to now?" she asked, sorting through the sandwiches, trying to avoid the sight of his naked chest, and the low-slung jeans that bared about as much as her heart could take.

"How about a nap?" Rafe murmured.

"Here? Now? You must be kidding?"

Not only was he *not* kidding, he was already snoring lightly.

Surprised, Maggie leaned back against a tree. *Go right ahead*, she thought, watching the rise and fall of Rafe's long body as she munched on a carrot. I don't mind a little eye candy. At liberty, she allowed herself a closer look at the man who was at once so appealing and yet so distant.

Was *that* what they called a six-pack? And that thick mat of black hair, a black whorl that disappeared beneath the zipper of his jeans. Those brawny forearms won by years of farming. Huge hands clasped behind his head. In his natural state, even the deep, weathered lines that creased Rafe's cheeks were beautiful. Beautiful, too, his mouth, a generous smile in repose, not the usual grimace to which she was more accustomed.

And he had laughed. *She* had made him laugh, and the sound had scored through her head and settled there as if it belonged.

Before she knew it she drifted off to sleep, until her rude awakening, occasioned by Rafe's noisy battle with the picnic basket. Battling to open her eyes, Maggie tried to get her bearings as Rafe stuffed the basket with the remnants of their meal.

"Sorry, Doc, but I've been trying to wake you for ten minutes. The sun is about to set."

"Ten minutes? I never sleep that heavily!"

Rafe was already headed back to his truck, the wicker basket in tow. "I fell asleep too, way too long, so come on, Maggie, I've got to pick up Amos on the way home and it's getting dark. He'll wonder where I am."

The ride back was quiet, a little unnerving for Maggie in the aftermath of their swim, but not unpleasant. She had things to think about, and guessed that Rafe did, too. Luckily, Amos was a great leveler to their budding romance. He came bounding down the steps of his friend's house even before Rafe put on the brakes. He seemed hard put, though, to decide who he was more excited to see—his dad, or Maggie.

Back in the truck, rumbling down the road, Maggie was glad when Rafe finally pulled up to Louisa's motel. Her brief nap in the woods had left her oddly more tired, and the swim in the pond left her longing for a shower.

"I won't be able to do this again for another few days," Rafe said as Maggie climbed from the truck. "I've got things that need tending."

"You've ignored things for me, haven't you?" Maggie said, feeling a bit guilty at taking up his time.

"Some."

"Is there anyone who can stand in for you?"

"It's a busy time of year for everyone," Rafe said, unsure if he wanted anyone else to escort her. "If you're not planting, you're harvesting, if you're not harvesting, you're fixing some piece of machinery, or waiting for the snow to melt, or the rain to stop," Maggie said as she removed her supplies from the truck. "Good night, Amos."

"'Night, Doctor Tremont."

"Young Amos," she said, tussling his hair, "every time I see you, you're about to fall asleep. Is my company so boring?" she teased.

"I think you're wonderful!" Amos said, earning surprised looks from the adults as he lay his sleepy head down on the seat.

"I think you're pretty special yourself," Maggie whispered gruffly. Ten minutes later, she too was falling asleep, dreaming of irascible farmers.

* * *

It took Maggie two days to organize a mini clinic that would operate from the cabin adjacent to hers. When Louisa had offered her the cabin, she'd accepted with alacrity. It did mean giving the cabin a complete scrubbing, and setting up a rough form of an office, but she managed to pull it off quite nicely, she thought, as she surveyed the cabin when she was done. It was certainly preferable to operating out of the back of the van, which is what she and her fellow doctors usually did.

But getting the word out was another matter. The morning of the third day, with no patients in sight, Maggie coaxed Louisa into giving her directions to Rafe's farm. After only one wrong turn, Maggie was relieved to come in sight of a small log cabin about eleven miles up the road, just as Louisa had promised. Amos stood on the porch, waving wildly when he recognized her van.

Neatly graveled, the path to the front door was bordered by a rough rock garden. The lawn was newly mowed and the porch was freshly painted, a neat extension to a carefully constructed log cabin. The Burnsides obviously took great pride in their home. But the apple trees were everything—and everywhere. Planted to the left of the house, planted to the right, neatly bedded in strict rows, severely trimmed to grow low (no doubt in concession to easier harvesting), they were the dominant visual of the farm. To the right side stood a huge red barn, also painted fairly recently, and next to that, a paddock where two cows grazed.

"Amos, what a nice hello! Is this your dog?" she said, scratching the ears of a short-haired yellow dog who greeted her almost as happily as his master.

"Her name is Tyla," Amos said proudly.

"A very pregnant Tyla," Maggie laughed, taking note of Tyla's bulging belly.

"Yeah, she's due any day. I can't wait till she has her puppies! Dad says we have to give them away, but I'll still get to play with them for a while. I'm hoping he'll let me keep at least one pup, so Tyla doesn't get lonely for her babies."

"Do you think I could have one, Amos?" Maggie was shocked to hear herself ask. But the minute she said it, she knew it was right. She *did* want a dog, she always had, even if she could not say when the idea was born.

Amos was almost as surprised as she. "Would you take good care of it?"

"She would get the very best," Maggie promised solemnly.

"I would have to ask my dad."

"Ask Dad what?" Rafe asked, as he strolled into view, wiping his hands on a dirty rag. Oil-slicked, Maggie judged from the smell.

"Hello, Rafe."

"Doctor Tremont." He nodded, surprising Maggie with his formality.

"Dad, Maggie says she wants one of Tyla's puppies."

"Does she, now?"

"Yes, she does." Maggie smiled, determined not to be put off by Rafe's bad mood. "If you and Amos think I have the makings of a good mom, I would love one."

"You probably would be," Rafe said thoughtfully. "But what brings you to this neck of the woods? Nobody sick that I know of."

"Nobody sick that I know of, either," Maggie grinned. "Louisa rented me a cabin, so I've set up a temporary clinic there. So less cramped than the van. But I haven't had any visitors today. I was sitting around twiddling my thumbs when I remembered my offer to help you with chores in exchange for you showing me the back roads of Primrose. You held to your part of the bargain, so I thought I'd hold to mine."

"Did you hear that, Amos? Doctor Tremont has offered to help out on the farm today."

"I think it's a great idea!"

"Is that right?" Amusement spread across Rafe's face as he threw aside his dirty rag. "Well, what precisely were you offering to do, Doctor Tremont?"

Maggie flushed, but stood her ground. Rafe was trying to intimidate her—and he was succeeding—but she was darned if she would let him know. "Whatever farm things you gentlemen think needs getting done," she said sweetly.

Rafe smiled. He liked the way she wouldn't back down, the way she looked like butter wouldn't melt in her mouth. Well, they'd see about that. "Can you milk a cow?"

Maggie's mouth turned down in a pout of good humor. "You know darned well that the closest I've ever been to a cow is the dairy section of the supermarket."

"Good, because that chore was done hours ago. Let's see. Can you clear brush?"

Hearing Amos giggle, she stared at Rafe with suspicion.

"Brush? Hmm. Perhaps if you picked something I might know about, or could do without much learning... What were *you* just doing? Maybe I could help with that."

"I was working on an old tractor, but I suppose you could hold the light," he mused, "since I don't expect you know anything about tractors. Do you know anything about tractors?"

"Not a thing."

"I thought not. Well, there *is* that load of hay I was hoping to move before the weekend."

"But Dad, I thought—"

"I changed my mind, Amos," Rafe said, staring at Maggie. "That's the perfect job for Doctor Tremont. You don't have to know much to move hay from one side of the barn to the other."

"But Dad, I thought—"

"You thought wrong, son. Now go on back in the house and finish washing up those breakfast dishes. And don't forget to sweep the floor this time."

Mumbling something about seeing Maggie later,

Amos headed for the house, Tyla doing a slow waddle as she followed her master. In silence, Rafe led the way to the barn, where they stood in the doorway together while their eyes adjusted to the dim, cavernous interior. In the far corner stood a battered tractor, an overhead light telling her that this was where Rafe had spent the morning. There were engine parts of all sizes strewn on a makeshift work bench, a tire sat propped against a wall and tools of varying import were strewn on the ground. Calling the vehicle a tractor was generous. It looked more valuable for its parts than anything else. And Maggie was sure she should not say so.

The hay Rafe intended her to move was in the loft. Climbing a sturdy ladder, he led her up to the loft and a stack of baled hay piled as high as it could get. Maggie wondered how he thought she could reach the top, much less lug the hay to the other side of the barn. He nodded toward a pitch fork.

"The idea is to move the bales as close to that door as possible so that we can slide them down the ramp without trouble. When winter comes, it's a bit of a chore when we have to do both, *and* get Amos to school on time. Not to mention it gets pretty cold here, in February. You can leave it piled low, I don't expect miracles from a lightweight like you. I'll stack it myself later in the week. Some of it will be going out to one of the sheds, but that will come later. For now, it would be a big help if you just moved it as I asked."

Maggie took a deep breath. There had to be at least thirty bales. "Okay, I can do that."

"Good. I'll do one for you, show you how it's done, then you're on your own. I'll be working on the tractor down below if you need me."

"I think I can handle a few bales of hay," Maggie said lightly.

Maggie watched as Rafe jabbed the pitchfork into a small bale and lifted it into the air. In a few steps, he was standing by the loft door and lowering the hay to the ground.

"Piece of cake," Maggie said nonchalantly as she reached for the pitchfork.

"Really? Then I'll leave you to your work. And Maggie, this was mighty nice of you to offer."

Maggie was so surprised at Rafe's thanks that she had to take a closer look to see if he was laughing. She could have sworn he had just wiped a grin off his face, but when she looked, he was his old, frowning self.

"Do the best you can. I don't expect miracles. I'll be in shouting distance, if you need me."

Maggie watched as Rafe disappeared below stairs. Left alone in the hay loft, Maggie eyed the hay stacked against the wall. Not impossible. Something about this was familiar, she thought, as she studied the barn. *Right!* This was *exactly* like that fairy tale where the girl was locked in a room and told to spin straw into gold! *Rumpelstiltskin!* Except there was no little man to rescue her. On the contrary...

"Everything okay up there?" she heard Rafe call.

She eyed the huge, iron pitchfork with dismay.

The darned thing weighed more than she did. "Just getting my bearings," she called back cheerfully.

Grabbing the pitchfork, she faced the bales with a grimace. But a promise was a promise. Valiantly, she stabbed at a bale but her effort went unrewarded. The fork didn't make a dent, the hay didn't move. She stabbed hard, but again, nothing. This was apparently going to be more difficult than it looked. Maybe if she pulled them down from the top, they would tumble a few feet. Yes, that seemed to work. Good. Now she could begin *hauling* it toward the loft door, maybe pushing it…except… What was that noise? Four mice ran from their hidey hole beneath the straw and scurried across the loft.

Maggie screamed so hard and so loud, and jumped so fast, that she fell back, landing hard on her rump. Terrified, she scrambled to her feet and leaped onto a guard rail just as Rafe clambered up the ladder.

"What the hell?" he cried, grabbing her legs before she fell and broke her neck. "What happened? Are you all right?"

Terrified beyond thought, Maggie leaped into his arms and buried her nose in his shirt. "*Mice!* You have bloody *mice!*" she shrieked, shaking like a leaf.

Above her, sight unseen, Rafe had to bite his lips to keep from laughing, but his voice, when he could finally speak, was a stern reprimand. "Damn it, woman, of course we have mice! This *is* a *bloody* barn!" But startled to find Maggie nestled in his arms, Rafe was suddenly in no hurry to return to his tractor.

The contours of her soft, womanly body and the delightful sensation of her heaving breasts were far more interesting than the repair of a broken axle.

"It's all right. They're only field mice and this is their natural habitat. But if so many scattered, I'm sure you won't find any more."

"You promise?" she asked into the flannel of his shirt.

"I can't *promise*." Rafe sighed, more for her unwitting assault on his heart than the guarantee she sought. "You probably scared them half to death, and anyway, did you notice the cats? That's why they're here."

Relaxing within the shelter of his arms, Maggie eyed the three tabbies blinking down at her from atop a roof beam. "What good are they doing sitting up there?" she grumbled.

"Ever hear about barn cats?"

Maggie hesitated. "In a story I once read."

"Tell me, Maggie, why do you think they live in barns? For the cheese?"

"Well, they're not doing a very good job. Besides, you could have warned me," she protested. "I thought cows lived in barns. I could do a cow... Maybe even a horse—*one horse*. But mice! Ugh!"

"If you want to stop, I'll understand."

"No!" Twisting in his arms, Maggie pushed Rafe away. That would amount to admitting to failure, something she would not do! The pitying way he looked at her, Maggie was ready to bash Rafe on the head with the pitchfork. And she didn't like one bit the way his shoulders were shaking. If she didn't know better, she would say he *was* laughing. But raising his hands, palms high, Rafe acceded to her wish and disappeared down the ladder for the second time.

Her jaw set firmly, Maggie turned back to the hay. Four mice were gone, that much she knew. The thing was, was the rest of the family still there? They *did* live in family groups, didn't they? *In nests*, if she remembered her biology. *Nasty, dirty little nests!* She took a step toward the ladder and stopped. No, she wasn't going to ask. She had already made a fool of herself. Ugh! This was disgusting! Warily, she eyed the hay stack from a number of angles, and poked at it until she convinced herself that it was rodent-free. Gritting her teeth, she stabbed at a bale with her pitchfork.

"Be careful not to stab yourself with the pitchfork" she heard him call. "I wouldn't want a lawsuit on my hands."

It was just as well he did not hear her curse.

Grumbling at the insensitivity of men, Maggie worked on for an hour with no more surprises, until the pitchfork, heavy to begin with, seemed exceedingly cumbersome and unwieldy. Sitting down to catch her breath, she wished she had thought to bring a bottle of water. Pride forbade her asking for one, although as a doctor, she knew that was the stupidest thing—dehydration, and all. As it was, she was sweating like a pig.

"Hey up there, how's it going?"

"Fine, just fine," Maggie murmured as she leaned

against a hay rick and closed her eyes with a deep sigh. It was just for a moment. After all, she was still recuperating from the flu, wasn't she? All that work, she thought, her eyelids flickering, and it seemed there was just as much hay piled in the corner as there was when she first started. Maybe she *should* help work on the tractor. Hold the light, or hand Rafe his tools, maybe. But she hated to give him the satisfaction of knowing she was exhausted, especially when she'd only been working a little over an hour. Holey moley, what her poor arms were going to feel like tomorrow she didn't want to think. She didn't want to think about *anything*, not even the way the hay was scratching her bare legs and working its way down the back of her shirt.

She had only been lying there a minute—surely not more!—when she felt something tickle her nose. Waving it away, she turned on her side and curled into a comfortable ball.

"G' way," she mumbled, but it refused to leave. She could feel it tickle her neck, then riff down her bare arm, bringing goose bumps to her skin. Opening her eyes, she saw Rafe squatting beside her, waving a bouquet of hay.

"You should see your hair," he smiled. "It's a real sorry mess."

"You don't have to sound so happy about it." But he was right. Pulling twigs of hay from her thick curls hair was hopeless. "Christ, I must be a sight."

"Yes, quite a sight," Rafe murmured.

Drawn by the curious quality of his voice, Maggie raised her eyes to find him staring hard at her.

"Look," he said gruffly, "I've been thinking...I really would like to kiss you."

Her eyes growing large, Maggie gasped. "That is definitely not a good idea."

"I think we should get it over with," he said, as if she hadn't spoken.

Get it over with? Now, there was an invitation!

Rafe shook his head with pained tolerance. "Doc, you have been a downright nuisance to my peace of mind."

"I'm sorry to be such an inconvenience." Maggie sniffed, as she scooted back against the wall of hay. "If you would just help me up, I would be on my way."

But Rafe was of no mind to do that. Grabbing hold of Maggie's ankle, with one swift tug he had Maggie flat on her back—and he looming above her, imprisoning her with his arms. "How pretty, all these red curls," he murmured, as he reached for a stray lock and rolled it between his fingers.

"Even covered in straw?" she asked bashfully.

"Especially covered in straw," he murmured, his expression serious as he plucked a stalk from her hair.

Valiantly, Maggie tried to ignore his hand as he ran his fingers through her hair. So gentle, but the response that trammeled through her body was a shock wave. When he pressed his lips to trace the shell of her ear, his moist breath warming her... If she had ever imagined what he must feel like, she now knew. It was not the sun she felt burning her cheeks, but the heat of his long arms as he drew her closer. His tongue tracing her mouth, shut tight against his onslaught, Maggie felt his smile against her resistance. "Come on, Doc, aren't you just a little curious? I know you are!" he murmured, nibbling at the corner of her mouth. "Come on, Maggie, put your arms around my neck."

"I—"

"Maggie, you talk too much."

Maggie felt his lips search out the faint pulse at her throat and travel her collar bone.

"Kiss me, Maggie," she heard him whisper as he shifted his weight to lie between her legs. His tongue darting to find hers was a challenge to her self-control. His taste was a fusion of coffee and sugar, his scent a tantalizing mix of sweat and machine oil and green grass. Maggie closed her eyes and gave in to the heady combination. Almost an imprint, his kiss was deep, smothering and demanding. Then, as suddenly as it began, cool air swept across her body and told her he was gone.

"Now, aren't you glad that's over and done with?" Rafe asked, his face unreadable as he scrambled to his feet. Putting out his hand, Rafe hauled her to her feet just in time to hear Amos running through the barn door.

"Maggieeeeeeeeee!" they heard Amos call.

"Hey, son, that's a lot of noise you're making," Rafe called back, his eyes never leaving Maggie. "Is everything okay?"

"Louisa just called. She says to remind Doctor Tremont that the clinic is supposed to reopen at four o'clock and to come home *right now*."

"Okay, son," Rafe called back. "She'll be down in a minute. We're just finishing up the last of the hay."

"Here, allow me." Flicking the last of the straw from Maggie's hair, Rafe stood back to admire his handiwork. Yes, that woman looked thoroughly kissed! Oddly pleased, he bent to plant a quick kiss on her swollen mouth, then nodded toward the ladder.

"Can I come with you?" Amos begged as Maggie's feet touched the ground. "My chores are done and I wouldn't be in the way. I could help, you know. Get you things."

"You could, hmm?" Maggie said, finding it hard to smile for the storm she was trying to calm within her. "Well, it's fine with me, but it's up to your dad."

Rafe shrugged. "It's up to *you*, Doc, but if you don't mind, I suppose I could pick him up later."

Maggie looked at Amos. "You look like you would make a good nurse, if you followed directions."

"Oh, I would, I would!" Amos promised.

"Well, then, let's go." Maggie smiled. "If we hurry, I can just fit in a shower."

And as Maggie hurried down the road, she missed the satisfied smile on Rafe's lips as he admired the gentle sway of her hips.

Chapter Six

Louisa Haymaker had done a good job getting the word out to Primrose. That evening, Maggie had two patients! She cleaned an infected wound, doled out antibiotics and was grateful for a smile. Both patients required follow-up visits, but when she urged them to follow up at the hospital in Bloomville, their smiles were noncommittal. It was her strong sense it was not going to happen. Was it their busy schedule? Inertia? The high price of gas? She didn't know, but it worried her.

For three long, hot summer days Maggie tended to patients and through it all, Amos was her staunch ally, Rafe having agreed to drive him down to town to help her. Greeting his neighbors, introducing them to

Maggie, Amos reassured people simply with his sunny smile. But she really had to respect his interest in medicine. He simply could not stop asking questions. Maybe he *would* go on to be a doctor, Maggie thought.

Rafe, however, remained an enigma. In no way, shape or form did he refer to their kiss, although Maggie thought of it often. She searched his eyes, tried to read his body language (even the tilt of his hat) but came up empty every time. Finally, she shrugged away the memory, as best she could. If that's how he wanted to play things, well, she was told she played a mean game of poker.

Since Rafe would not allow Maggie to pay Amos for his help at the clinic, she asked if she could take the boy on an outing instead. For pizza, over in Bloomville, and if Rafe allowed, a movie. If Rafe wanted, he was invited to accompany them. He said no so loudly that the whole county must have heard. But he called back to say yes, an hour later. Amos could hardly contain himself. They set the date for Sunday, when the clinic would be closed. And besides, it was going to rain. Perfect weather for a movie, Maggie promised Amos.

"And hot, buttered popcorn?" he asked shyly.

"Hot, buttered popcorn and a large soda!" Maggie promised.

It was raining Sunday, a steady drizzle, just like the weatherman promised, when they all set out for the hour-long drive. But this time Maggie was prepared. Muggy though it was, she wore her work boots to keep her feet dry, and draped a cream-colored fisherman's cable sweater around her shoulders, and had dredged up her long-lost umbrella from the back of her van. She would not court another cold. She let Rafe drive, too, no argument there, and noticed, as she fastened her seat belt, that he was freshly shaved and smelled of aftershave. And she was pretty sure that Amos was wearing some of his dad's aftershave, too! It wasn't hard to tell the importance of this adventure to the boy and she was glad to have thought up the trip.

An hour's drive to the other side of the mountain was the other side of the moon to Amos. She wondered if this weren't true for Rafe, too. It was a special event, even if he denied it. If she had asked what the last movie was he had seen, she'd bet anything he would say something like *Casablanca*. Maggie herself had never been in Bloomville but when they came within five miles of the town, houses started to appear, sporadically, at first, then in clusters that told they were very close. A town populated by four thousand people rendered Bloomville a small city. It even sported a strip mall. Amos was so excited that Maggie suspected he could skip the movie and head straight into the mall, the mall probably more a curiosity to Amos than an opportunity to shop.

They arrived at the theater in plenty of time to secure good seats and allow Amos to buy popcorn. Settling back in their seats, the little boy sitting between them, Maggie glanced over his head to see how Rafe was handling the trip. Good lord, did the man *never* smile, she wondered as she glanced at his unsmiling silhouette. The way he was taking in the theater, looking up, looking down, checking out the other patrons, you'd think he'd never been to a movie. But the rowdy amusement of a bunch of teens in the back row made even Amos turn his head. Maggie could tell by the boy's close observation that he was monitoring their uninhibited behavior and measuring it against his own restricted upbringing, a fact for which Rafe would not thank her. Living in Boston, she was used to kids being loud and boisterous. That's what teenagers did to get attention. It didn't mean that Amos would behave like that. But it meant that Rafe would worry about it.

The movie was a crazy comedy that Amos and Maggie loved, and made Rafe wince. But when Amos saw the posters of future movies, as they left the theater, and asked if they could return to see them, Rafe didn't say no. They found a pizza place that met all Amos's requirements. The smell of fresh tomato sauce and garlic was so enticing it made Maggie's mouth water, too. In minutes they were huddled together in a shiny, red vinyl booth. Before Rafe could stop her, Maggie ordered a large pie with extra cheese, and a basket of garlic knots, sure that a man his size would do justice to the meal, no matter what he said.

What were garlic knots? Amos wanted to know.

You'll see, Maggie promised with a wide grin.

Will I like them?

Oh, yes!

Watching Amos try to negotiate a cheesy slice of pizza, Maggie realized with a pang that she did not spend enough time with children. Oh, she couldn't begin to count the children she treated in her practice, but to be sitting here with Amos was an unlooked for delight. Did she regret not having children? The thought crossed her mind, as it had over the years, oh, maybe four million times. Twice she had even started the process for adopting, but it always seemed to fizzle out. Her work always seemed to take precedence so that eventually her work took the place of family. It had been that insight, not six months ago, which caused her to reassess her priorities. That if she didn't have a husband and kids, she was still entitled to more than the role of designated *auntie* at her friends' family parties.

And there she was sitting with Rafe, a man who had a son in whom he seemed to take little joy. If that was true. *Was* he as grumpy around Amos as his public persona implied? No, it wasn't Amos who made him unhappy—how could that be—it was something else. The weight of the world kind of stuff. Amos was probably the only bright spot in Rafe's life, judging from the way he watched the boy, the effort he made for the child, the smiles they shared, even if he was the grumpiest man she had ever met.

And the most interesting. Now, why was that? What made this man so compelling? It couldn't be his conversation, that was for sure. Certainly not his looks. You could make a map of his scars, so she knew it wasn't his looks. Well, but his eyes, now that was a different matter. Deep-set brown eyes, so dark they almost seemed black, shadowed by the raw deal life had dealt him. So burdened that the simplest pleasures seemed beyond him. Some people made lemonade out of lemons, she thought. Not Rafe, although she was beginning to suspect there was a lot of hot air in his balloon. Especially when she glanced down at his plate, not a scrap of food remaining.

"You look like a little boy with that sauce on your face," she said, leaning across the table to dab at the corner of his mouth.

"Thank you," he said. "I hate to say it, Doc, but this was a good idea."

Maggie smiled. "I hoped you would enjoy the day as much as the little man beside you."

Amos grinned as he polished off the last of his soda. "This is the best day of my life!" he chirped happily.

"You mean a walk through the mall couldn't make it any better?" Maggie teased.

Amos's eyes grew wide, but then he remembered Rafe. "Could we, Dad? Do we *have* to go home right away?"

Maggie watched as Rafe mulled it over. The poor man, his face was such an open book. What did he want, anyway? How much did he think he owed to a life of abstinence? Was he into punishing himself? If so, for what? A wayward wife?

The hard luck to raise this wonderful son alone? Or was it something she knew nothing about? What did it take to make him laugh?

And why did she care? Now, *there* was a question!

"Ready for that walk, then? Rafe?"

"I guess," he said, throwing his balled napkin on the platter.

Maggie smiled. "Oh, come on, Rafe, you don't have to *buy* anything. Window shopping can be fun. You do know how to spell fun, don't you?"

"Yes, but I spell it a Sunday afternoon nap on the sofa."

"Well, if you're that tired, I'll be glad to drive home while you nap in the truck."

"Right! Like I'm suicidal!"

"Mr. Burnside, are you being sexist?" Maggie asked, her brows raised.

"Sexist?"

"I'm asking because you're talking like I haven't been driving for over twenty years, so I have to wonder what makes you say such a thing. Is it because I'm a woman?"

Rafe didn't even blush. "What would that have to do with it?"

"Then why did you say that?"

"Well, if you recall, you *did* get lost looking for Bloomville. That's the only reason you found Primrose. It's not like you looked on a map or followed any road signs."

"Primrose isn't on the map, if you recall! And as

for road signs, the only one I saw was hardly legible."

But Rafe did not want to talk about Primrose and its problems. He wasn't sure he even wanted Primrose on a map. And he sure didn't want to listen to Maggie talk about markets and meetings and the development of his village. Look what happened over in Bloomville. When they started advertising online, so many tourists invaded, the next thing you knew they had built a hotel, constructed a ski lift, and everyone was buying satellite dishes! He and Doctor Tremont were on different wavelengths when it came to civic improvement. Not that he blamed her. The problems Louisa had told Maggie about the town were true, and they were things he worried about, too. But the preservation of the White Mountains was important. He just didn't know how to negotiate the two, and he did not want to be rushed into making decisions that would be irrevocable.

Women did that. Women made snap decisions, and too bad for anyone who stood in their way. And once a thing was done, there was no going back. Hadn't he seen Rose do it? And worse, his ex-wife hadn't cared one jot for the baby she'd left behind, once she made up her mind to leave. If Maggie was careless like that, it could be harmful to Primrose, and worse, she would not be there to pick up the pieces. Not that she didn't mean well. He was sure her intentions were good. But that was no guarantee of anything. And it wasn't the sort of thing he wanted to argue about, not on this special day, so he hurried from the pizza parlor and beckoned her to follow.

It was nice to walk down the softly lit mall with Rafe and Amos, Maggie decided. When people glanced at Amos and smiled, Maggie felt a surge of pride, almost as if he were her own. She certainly felt that way whenever he took her hand to drag her through a store. Sharing his enthusiasm was an unlooked for pleasure. And the significance of his hand clasp was not lost on Rafe.

"So, when are you leaving Primrose?" he asked as they watched Amos wander up and down the aisles. The way Maggie's face fell, Rafe was sorry the minute the words were out of his mouth.

"I'm sorry, Maggie. That was incredibly rude of me. I didn't mean it the way it sounded."

Maggie stiffened. She couldn't seem to reconcile the man who kissed her in the hay loft with the man who acted like she was the worst thing to happen to Primrose.

"I just don't understand you. You've been rude, boorish and a general pain in the butt. Even when you took me up the mountain to offer people medical care, you were a terrible companion. All I wanted was to help rectify a mistake. Even now, all I want is for Amos to have a nice day, but you…you look like you just left the dentist's office!"

Rafe turned crimson. "That good, huh?"

But Maggie wasn't satisfied. "Is there any winning with you, Mr. Burnside?"

Rafe hesitated. "I guess I *could* be more polite."

"It would be a start."

"I really have got your dander up, haven't I?"

"And I don't find it funny."

"I wasn't joking, I don't know how to joke. I wish I did, maybe it would help. All I know is that the other day, in the hay loft, when I kissed you, I was hoping to get you out of my system, but it seems all I want is to do it again."

Now it was Maggie's turn to blush. "It may come as a surprise to you, Mr. Burnside, but some people actually *like* to be kissed."

"Oh, I liked kissing you. Maybe too much. I get to making it a habit, one day you'll be gone, then where will I be?"

"At square one?" Maggie regretted her outburst as soon as she spoke. Rafe was only trying to be honest with her. "Sorry. My turn to be rude. But you know the old saw—*nothing ventured, nothing gained.*"

"And what do I have to gain?" Rafe growled.

"The simple pleasure of a kiss?" Maggie suggested.

The ride home was quiet, not the least because Amos fell asleep before they had even gone five miles. Maggie liked the silence, the soothing quiet of the drive, liked the confident way Rafe controlled the road. She liked, too, peeking through the brightly lit windows of the homes they passed, catching a quick glimpse of a moving body, or the flickering blue light of a television screen. Then it was completely dark, and all she could see was the road directly ahead, lit by the high beams of Rafe's truck. It wasn't long before he was shaking *her* awake.

"Amos and I always seem to be falling asleep on you," Maggie observed with a small smile as she blinked away her cat nap. Careful not to wake the sleeping boy, she slid from the truck and whispered Rafe good night.

"Wait. I'll walk you to your door," he said quietly.

"No need. It's not far."

"When a man offers to see you to your door, Doctor Tremont, you should take him up on the offer."

"Oh… Okay then…"

"Right. And when a man wants to kiss you good night you should take him up on that offer, too."

"Oh!"

"The simple pleasure of a kiss," Rafe whispered as he took her in his arms.

His lips pressed to hers, Rafe kissed Maggie lightly. Raising his head, he gazed into her eyes then pressed another soft kiss to her forehead. "*Now* we can say good night."

Walking back to his truck, Rafe could feel Maggie's eyes on his back. If it weren't for Amos, he would have asked if he could stay. His desire for this woman surprised him with its intensity. He hadn't been looking, but somehow the moment he saw her standing in the middle of Louisa's gas station, bedraggled and wet, his heart had taken an unexpected lurch. Well, that was what you got for trying to be nice, because for sure, he did not want to take the blame for this unexpected turn of events! Sure, he had no problem kissing her. Wasn't that what their little tryst in the hay loft had been about? And damned if it hadn't crossed his mind to take her then and there if Amos hadn't been about. But more fool him, the silly kiss had only left him hankering for more. So tonight, he kissed her again. *Just to see*, he told himself. So, why, then, did he feel an urgent need to kiss this woman breathless? It was a puzzle he did not have an answer to, even as he put his son to bed later that night.

The next day was a long one for Maggie, because she simply could not erase the memory of last night's scene from her mind. How a simple kiss could prove such a distraction was beyond her. The man had hardly touched her! Why, then, did thoughts of Rafe Burnside encroach at the most impossible times? When she examined her few patients, she was all business, but when she was in between examinations, filling her supply trays or cleaning her instruments, all she could think of was Rafe. The most nonsensical thoughts, too! *Maggie Tremont*, she berated herself, *what are you doing, falling in love?* That thought, unbidden, was enough to make her drop her stethoscope. *Falling in love?* That was not on her agenda. She had all but given up in *that* direction. She was just this side of forty, for goodness' sake! *This* wasn't how it was supposed to happen! One fell in love with that damned prince at the ball—or a reasonable facsimile—*not* a mud-splattered farmer who had the temperament of a grizzly bear!

Her thoughts were full of impassioned italics all morning, and her stethoscope trembled in her hand right up to the moment Rafe appeared with Amos at the clinic. She had no idea how to behave. Be embarrassed or friendly? Which? But Rafe took care of that in his own laconic way.

"Amos and I would like to invite you to dinner this evening."

More Amos than you, Maggie thought dryly. "Why thank you, Amos. That would be wonderful."

"Don't count on anything special."

"Whatever you make works for me." Maggie smiled. "I am the world's worst cook."

"I'm sure you do other things well," Rafe said, with a face so expessionless Maggie didn't know if he was joking until she remembered that he didn't joke.

It was a light afternoon for seeing patients, so Maggie and Amos packed it in around four and drove up to the cabin, where they found Rafe grilling chicken. At the sight of her master, Tyla went wild.

"Hey, you good girl," Amos fussed as he bent to scratch his dog's huge belly.

"How is she doing?" Maggie asked, kneeling down beside Amos and Tyla. "She looks a lot bigger than last week. She must be due any minute."

"Dad thinks so, too, so we set up a corner in the barn for her to give birth."

"Right now, she looks as if she's due for her dinner," Maggie chuckled as she rose to her feet. "Mr. Burnside, that chicken smells wonderful."

"Anyone can barbecue."

"Louisa didn't seem to know that you could cook so well. She was surprised when I told her you had brought me a Scotch broth when I was sick."

"She knows I cook a little. I feed her often enough, don't I? I just don't make a big deal of it."

"Not a real man's job?"

Rafe shrugged. "Not what I was taught a man should be, but then, I never intended to be a father *and* a mother. But things don't always work out how you planned. On the other hand, sometimes they work out better," he said, ruffling Amos's hair as he joined them.

"Amos," Maggie said, smiling, "what do you think? Has your dad been a good mom?"

Amos smiled back. "Yeah, pretty good except when he burns the toast at breakfast. Then he's more like a dad. He cusses real good."

Rafe smiled as he removed the chicken from the grill. "Hey, guy, I've heard you say a few words I didn't know you knew, when you didn't think I was around."

Listening to their good natured banter, Maggie followed them up the porch steps to discover a table laid for three.

"We thought you might enjoy eating on the porch. It's cooler than the house."

"So pretty," Maggie murmured as she took her

seat. The plates were unmatched, the silverware was badly scratched, but a small vase of bluebells and buttercups that had obviously been picked that day lit up the center of the table.

"Oh, Rafe, this is so nice. Thank you," she said. "It's been an age since I was entertained."

"Amos picked the flowers this morning, before we left for your place. He wouldn't leave until he did."

"Oh, Amos, thank you! They're lovely. You must have been awfully sure I would come."

Amos blushed. "I hoped you would. Dad said your dance card probably wasn't that full. What's a dance card?"

"In the old days, a dance card was a sort of an appointment book, but for a dance. And your dad was right," she laughed. "I have none. Hey, while I'm here, do you think I could get a quick tour of your house? I didn't get a chance to see your room the last time I was here."

"Sure," Amos said, pleased by her request. "Right after dinner. My room is the nicest."

"I'm sure it is." Maggie smiled, as Rafe handed her a bowl of peas. "Freshly picked?"

Rafe nodded. "By the boy. Not his favorite job, though, right, Amos?"

"Then I'm doubly grateful."

Rafe asked Amos to light candles against the dimming light, and the result was so romantic and beautiful that Maggie never wanted to leave. They ate in amiable silence, passing the rolls and butter, shuffling the platter of chicken from one end of the table to the other, helping themselves to buttered peas. And as they ate, Maggie listened closely as Amos told her all about his school and his friends, and funny farm stories, while Rafe sat quietly, content to let his son have center stage. After dinner, when they all declared they could not take another bite, Maggie got her wished-for tour of the Burnside home.

The exterior might be classic log cabin, but the interior rough timber had been sheetrocked, and the floors laid with beautiful golden oak planks that reflected the soft patina of time. The furniture was nondescript American traditional, a bit on the shabby side; oversized, sturdy stuff that could handle a man Rafe's size and still withstand the abuse of a small child. It suited the Burnside men admirably. Hurricane lamps sat on battered end tables, but someone was reading *The Nation*, and it sure wasn't Amos, and that impressed Maggie more than anything else.

Maggie smiled when Amos opened the door to his sanctuary. He was right, it *was* the nicest room in the house because it reflected the abundant energy of a boy's life. Maggie was glad to see that Rafe's otherwise firm hand had allowed Amos the freedom of his privacy, because it looked like a tornado had swept through it. Posters of Bode Miller covered the walls, but she wasn't surprised—*this was New Hampshire, after all*—and Bode Miller was probably the next best thing to God, thereabouts.

"Do you know him?" Maggie asked as Amos showed her his ski trophies, and was not surprised when Amos answered in the affirmative.

"Bode? Of course! Everybody does! He skis over at Cannon. My dad is friends with his dad."

Which told her what the Burnsides did during the long winter months.

"That's where all our money goes," Rafe confirmed as he filled the doorway.

"Are you training Amos for the Olympics?"

"Ask him. He's been skiing ever since he was three, but skiing in the Olympics is a tall order. But since Bode skied in Turin, the boy's gotten ideas."

"Big ideas," Amos said, sending his dad a spirited look. "I have a savings account all my own for new skis and stuff, 'cause Dad pays me for doing chores. That's why I do so much. I have to buy all my ski stuff out of that money. Skis, boots, gloves, my jackets and stuff. Dad says I grow faster than the weeds on our front lawn. If I break a ski I'm in big trouble. But Bode gives me his old stuff, so that helps a lot."

"Your dad's right," Maggie said as they headed back downstairs. "Some of my young patients back in Boston, I don't recognize them, one visit to the next, they grow so fast."

Setting two mugs on the porch table, Rafe lit citronella candles against the mosquitoes, then he and Maggie sat down to share their coffee with the crickets. From where they sat, they could see Amos through a screen window, curled on the couch with a book. Tyla was asleep on his lap.

"A picture postcard for country living," Maggie said, with a smile. "You've done a great job raising him, Rafe."

"I did what I had to do."

"Still, you are one lucky guy to have a kid like that."

"I'm lucky to have *him*. He's what's kept me going all these years."

"You mean since—" Maggie paused, unsure what to say, how much to reveal what she knew about the Burnsides.

But Rafe knew what she meant. Nobody knew better than he how fast small town gossip traveled. "Since Rose left me, yes."

"She left Amos, too."

"And I don't know how she did it."

"Nonetheless, you did a splendid job with the boy. He's gentle, well-mannered, polite…"

"Sure, but he misses a mother's hand. I've tried to make up for it, but having a mother is…I don't know…softer. I don't know how else to explain it."

"You don't have to."

They sat quietly, enjoying the nightfall until Maggie roused herself to leave. "It's getting dark, I'd better get going." Tapping on the screen window, she beckoned to Amos. "I'm going, Amos. I have a long list of patients tomorrow. Will I be seeing you?"

She watched as Amos came to the screen window to say goodbye. "If my dad drives me." Amos looked at Rafe, a hopeful look in his eye.

Rafe smiled. "It seems to me, son, you may have medicine in your future."

Amos brightened. "I was thinking about being a vet, Dad. What do you think?"

"I think you're going to get some practice in way before you get your license, if Tyla's belly is any indication."

Chapter Seven

Tyla's pups decided to make their entrance into the world that very night, and she never made it to the barn, either. Tracking her odd mewling sound the next morning, Rafe and Amos found the new mother tucked beneath the sofa. The tired pooch eyed them with a combination of pride and suspicion, but they were wise enough in the ways of animals not to touch her pups. They did clean the area, though, and brought her food and water, but Tyla was more interested in sleeping, so they left her alone. Amos insisted on staying home to guard the puppies, but he did call Maggie to let her know what happened and invite her up to see the litter.

She arrived while Rafe was still in the field so that

when he came in to wash up, he was treated to the sight of her cute rump in the air, as she and Amos cooed at the new mother sheltering beneath the sofa. "This does not bode well for my dinner," he said, barely able to suppress a smile.

Startled, Maggie and Amos scrambled to their feet.

"How's she doing, Doc?"

"I'm not a vet, but it looks to me like mother and children are doing fine, and those pups are adorable. No hair, yet, of course, but as soon as they get some weight on them, Amos says I can pick one."

"They won't be able to separate from Tyla for at least six, maybe eight weeks. How are you going to pick it up, if you're not here?"

"No problem," she said breezily. "I'm sure I can get a few days leave to visit."

The way his mouth turned down, Maggie supposed that Rafe was none too pleased with her and quickly changed the subject. "I brought dinner. Actually, I brought Louisa," she admitted wryly. "She insisted on coming, but the way she's banging away with the pots and pans in your kitchen, I don't think you'll mind."

"I wondered what that noise was."

"Since I've been treating her legs, she's vastly improved, although some physical therapy wouldn't be a bad idea. I'm working on getting a physical therapist to come to town, maybe on a steady basis."

"How nice of you…" But the way Rafe said it, as he went upstairs to shower, Maggie couldn't be sure.

Dinner was excellent, but that was because Louisa was an excellent cook, which no one could stop telling her.

"You would think no one here ever ate before," she snorted as she passed the pot roast, but they could tell she was pleased by their compliments. "I've been thinking about starting a business. Baking pies, bottling sauces and jams and stuff. Fannie Congreve and I have been talking."

Quietly, Rafe laid down his fork.

"Frank thinks it would be good for Fannie to have something to do besides the kids, not to mention the extra income it could bring them. We started talking about it last year, when we bottled our winter preserves together. She's a fine cook, you know, she makes a terrific tomato chutney. Of course, I liked her blackberry preserves best, but I always did have a sweet tooth. Talking about sweet tooths," she winked at Amos, "I do believe I saw an apple pie cooling in the kitchen, if you've a mind to go bring it in."

His eyes gleaming, Amos leaped to his feet and ran to the kitchen to fetch the pie. With Amos out of the room, Louisa felt more at liberty to talk.

"With little miss here coming to town and bringing a breath of fresh air, Fannie and I have been thinking about it again. When Maggie ran around with you last week, I asked her to take a sort of informal survey if anyone else was interested. One hundred percent were interested! We were pretty surprised, but when we thought about it, it made sense. People are concerned about the future of their kids, Rafe, more so than their fear of change. But you know that better than I," she left off delicately.

Of course he did. He only had to look at his own son to know how much his neighbors worried about theirs. Watching Amos return with the apple pie, carefully balanced in two hands, he knew the weight of their worries.

"*That* says it all," Maggie said, grinning at the sight of the beautiful pie. "No one bakes like Louisa Haymaker. Traveling like I do, I've tasted enough pie to know what I'm talking about. It should be sold at the farmer's market."

"Come on, Maggie, this town can't set up a market just because Fannie Congreve got a bug."

"Why not?" she asked indignantly. "Practically every town in New England has one, so why not Primrose? You guys could make a fortune selling Louisa's pies. And how about Fannie's chutney and preserves, and Marybeth Hart's homemade bread, and Billie Temple's coleslaw, and—"

"Marybeth Hart's homemade bread and Billie Temple's coleslaw?" Rafe stopped her. "How did you come to hear about all that?"

"At the cabin clinic. Rafe, every woman who came to the clinic was taken by the idea. There was even mention of starting a restaurant. And why the heck not? There isn't a restaurant. Louisa said if that happened, she wouldn't mind fixing up the motel a bit. And Shandie Whitehead said that if

Louisa did *that,* than she would give serious thought to opening a bed and breakfast. She said that with Elmer gone, the house seemed so big and empty… We said we would help her."

"*We?*"

"A figure of speech."

Amos was crestfallen. "But, Maggie, why can't you stay and help?"

"I told you, sweetie, I have a job to get back to."

"But Primrose needs a doctor, too, and everyone loves the clinic, so why can't you stay? I would help you. I've been a good worker, haven't I? And then you could teach me medicine, so I could become a doctor like you."

"That's quite a compliment, Amos."

"It's more than a compliment, Maggie," Louisa said firmly. "You have lit up the boy's life with possibilities, things he never thought about until you showed up. Amos is right. You could do worse than settle down in Primrose—if you've a mind to make a few changes, of course," she said with an impish smile.

The more Louisa spoke, the more Rafe grew quiet. The looks he kept darting at his son told a painful story. Did Amos's chatter about becoming a vet make Rafe uncomfortable? It might, if he had plans for his son to take over the farm. Maggie just hoped that Rafe wouldn't make her the fall guy for his anger. She sure hoped Louisa's apple pie had the magical power to sweeten his temper because it was getting pretty tense at the table. Only Amos didn't seem to notice, so she offered him the first piece, when she began to serve the pie.

"Oh, my goodness," Louisa cried, clapping her hands in dismay. "I almost forgot!"

Everyone froze, waiting for another bombshell to fall.

"Amos, child, go look in the freezer! I brought a container of my very own homemade ice cream. Vanilla, your favorite! I was saving it for a special event, and if this isn't it, I don't know what is."

"But what are we celebrating?" Amos asked, as he headed for the kitchen.

"New beginnings, child, new beginnings."

"It's nice being up here on the mountain, isn't it?" Louisa said, as she and Maggie drove home later that night. "Rafe has a beautiful piece of property, doesn't he?"

Louisa waited expectantly, but Maggie was too busy concentrating on the road to reply.

Wedged into the front seat for the ride home, Louisa leaned back and stretched her swollen legs with a grateful sigh. "It's been a while since I got out. My legs don't let me do the things I used to do. Not that you haven't helped them, the good lord knows, but I used to get in my car and drive for hours. Me and Frank Sinatra," she laughed.

"I know what you mean. For me it's Pink Floyd."

"Never heard of them."

"Don't worry." Maggie grinned. "They don't compare to Frank Sinatra."

The women enjoyed the rest of the ride down the mountain in companionable silence. No stranger to country roads, Maggie still took it slow, it was so dark. And she was always on the lookout for deer. Hitting one could cost you your car, not to mention your life and the deer's.

"My late husband, Jack, always wanted us to move down to Florida," Louisa revealed as the got to the end of the road. "He hated shovelling snow. But I wouldn't budge. The country always did cast a spell on me."

Louisa looked sideways at Maggie.

"This town needs someone like you, Maggie Tremont. You know that, don't you?"

"Perhaps," Maggie murmured.

"And *he* needs you just as much," Louisa added.

Maggie didn't play dumb. "I know that I like him very much."

"How much is *very much?*"

"I think…very much."

"Good!" Louisa said, satisfied with that answer. "Because *I* know he's sweet on you. He wouldn't be having a conniption if he weren't." she said sagely. "I know Rafe Burnside like the back of my hand. I changed his diapers when he was a baby. He's been caught off guard, is all. He just has to be convinced you're for his own good. He wasn't expecting a little thing like you, coming in out of the rain, looking like a dead rat…"

"Thank you so much for the compliment!"

"…catching him unawares. Making him fall in love."

"Fall in love?" Maggie screeched.

"Do you have a hearing problem, Doctor Tremont?" Louisa asked serenely, "because you keep repeating everything I say."

"I don't want to *convince* him," Maggie protested. "I wouldn't want to convince any man to...to...to want me! I want to be desired out of *affection*, not *persuasion!*"

"Doctor Tremont," Louisa said on a long sigh. "That poor man is suffering mightily. Most men do, when they fall in love. He is *not* likely to appreciate the value of a fine, young woman like yourself when he's in that state."

"He didn't need to be persuaded by Rose!"

"Ach! She doesn't count. She was his childhood love. He's a man, he thinks he knows everything, God save us all! He just needs to be re-educated. In my day we said handled," she wisecracked. "Whatever you modern women want to call it, a man like Rafe Burnside goes kicking and screaming to the altar."

"To the altar?" Maggie gasped.

"Wasn't that what we were talking about?" Louisa asked, wide-eyed and innocent.

"For Pete's sake, Louisa, I've only been here a few weeks! We were talking about a mutual attraction, not love!"

"You don't believe in love at first sight?" Louisa asked, matter-of-factly.

"In books, maybe!" Maggie snapped. "Good grief, Louisa, have you taken leave of your senses?"

Louisa was unperturbed. "Maybe, but I wouldn't mind seeing that boy married before I died. He deserves a little happiness, and you two are a perfect fit. Personally, I believe your arrival in Primrose was heaven-sent, for Rafe as well as the rest of us. Of course, I wouldn't push you, but if you were inclined in that direction, I wouldn't mind. As for Rafe, he's so busy planting apple seeds, he hasn't got time to think. It's up to us to help him see, is all. We just have to make him stand still first!"

Whatever Rafe might think about a farmer's market, it was an idea that was beginning to catch fire in Primrose. When Maggie stepped outside her cabin the next morning, there was a small contingent of women sitting on the grass, wanting to speak to her, Fannie Congreve included.

"Good morning, Maggie." Fannie smiled, the twins cooing beside her in a double stroller. "I brought the boys down for a check up, but they ran over to say hello to Louisa, probably stuffing themselves with cookies. I also arranged for you to meet some of my friends."

Fannie introduced Maggie to the three women who returned her greeting warmly. "It is a real kindness that you've been able to help us out," one woman said. "We know you didn't have to."

Maggie shook her head. "I didn't do anything you weren't entitled to."

Fannie shrugged. "Still, you didn't have to. We could have waited for the next visit of the medical van, or gone over to Bloomville and been done with it. You're a godsend though, especially for the children, and it was our conversation about the children that got us to thinking that we should stop dillydallying and do something about the town."

"Maybe do some of the things Fannie and Louisa have been suggesting about reviving the place," another woman said.

"Fannie came up with the idea of a farmer's market last fall, but we never did anything about it," the third woman explained. "With the harvest approaching in a couple of months, we thought maybe we should form a committee to see if it was something that could really happen."

"And it goes without saying we'd be glad to have your help."

"If I am responsible in any way for this," Maggie said, "I'm thrilled. And if I can help in any way, I certainly will."

"It would be better if you lived here…" Fannie said. "But since you don't…"

"No, I don't."

"But it's—"

"Food for thought," Fannie winked at her new friend.

Thus the Primrose Farmland Enterprise Committee was born. And when word got out, the committee of four grew to sixteen, and a planning meeting was set for the following Tuesday, to thrash out ideas to get the market off the ground. It was decided that the schoolroom would serve as headquarters, and when Maggie arrived Tuesday evening, it was standing room only.

The only fly in the ointment was Rafe Burnside, sitting quietly in the back row. His demeanor was so solemn that no one dared approach him, much less sit beside him. Giving him a quick nod, his friends moved on to find seats closer to the stage. But Maggie dared.

"Hi, cowboy," she greeted him cheerfully. "Traveling alone, tonight? I would have thought all this excitement would have got Amos's attention."

"He's spending the evening with the Congreves," Rafe told her, staring straight ahead. "We're sharing a babysitter."

"He probably made the right choice," Maggie said agreeably.

But try as she would, Rafe refused to be engaged. His attention was completely focused on the speakers clustered at the podium. If he liked what he heard, Maggie was hard put to tell, the look on his face was so remote. She knew quite well that one bad word from him could send the townsfolk into a tailspin—and their dreams for a farmer's market with it. But Rafe said nothing, and gave away nothing. He sat through the brainstorming session without making any comments as the committee thrashed out ideas—where to set up the market, what to sell, who to supply the preserves and baked goods, how to advertise the market. And how to pay for it, someone called out at one point, which made everyone laugh. There were so many ideas, so many things to think about, that it was close to ten before the room emptied out. Offering to drive Louisa home, the Congreves asked Maggie if she wanted a ride, too, but she decided to walk back to the motel with Rafe.

"This market will change everything," he said softly, leaves crunching beneath his boot heels as they headed back.

"Rafe," Maggie said, hearing the concern in his voice. "Primrose needs this. Primrose needs more than this, if the truth be told. But mostly, Primrose needs you."

"Me?" he scoffed.

"Yes, *you!*" Maggie insisted. "Didn't you see how everyone kept looking at you tonight, to see what you were thinking? They want your approval!"

"They don't need my approval."

"They don't *need* it, but they *want* it because, whether you like it or not, *you* are their standard bearer. They measure everything they do around what you might think. You lend authority and legitimacy to their enterprise. If you gave the market your blessing it would take off like a rocket."

"Primrose needs more than a farmer's market."

"They know that, but it's a start. I did mention to Fannie in passing that she might try to get some of the local congressmen from Albany to take an interest in the area. Maybe they could be persuaded to spend some of your tax dollars here."

"And how would she perform that miracle?"

"She starts slow, like everything else. Maybe she invites them to the opening of the farmer's market. Politicians adore getting their pictures taken. Then, while they're shaking hands and sipping Louisa's lemonade and smiling for the camera, they get cornered by some good ideas."

"And what's your part, Maggie?" Rafe asked as they marched down the dark road, their steps lit by the pale, yellow moon.

Maggie checked her steps. "I have no part, except the most marginal. I'm just passing through, remember? I lend them my support as an extension of my job."

"Damn it, Maggie, can I please get a straight answer?"

"Rafe, that *is* a straight answer. Isn't that enough, or have you forgotten how to accept a friendly hand?"

"Come on, Maggie, do you honestly think you're the first Samaritan who ever drove into Primrose with a shopping bag of ideas how to fix this broken town?"

"Yes, I think maybe I am!" she retorted.

"Well, you're not. We've had tons just like you. They land their feet in Primrose, stir everybody up, but they never stay. When they get tired of shoveling snow eight months a year, or not finding smoked cheese in the supermarket, they hurry back to their fancy restaurants and book stores—and malls, damn it, malls! And indoor heating is a real plus compared to a wood-burning stove in the middle of February. Let me tell you something, Doc, there's payment to be had for giving Primrose false hope, but you won't pay the price—we will!"

"I wouldn't do that!" Maggie protested. " How could you think so? What have I done to make you think I would be so callous?"

"Maybe you wouldn't mean it, but the outcome would be the same," Rafe said, his voice a cold lash on her heart.

Frustrated, Maggie searched for words to cut through the pain in his eyes. On impulse, she threw her arms around his neck.

Surprised, Rafe tried to throw her off, but Maggie clung to him tightly. "Is this one of your tricks, Doc?"

"I'm kissing you, Rafe Burnside, because words don't seem to work with you."

"Oh, I hear you, Maggie. It's *you* who doesn't hear *me*."

Molding his body to hers, Rafe kissed her with such fierce abandon that Maggie felt as if a veil had been dropped. *This,* she thought, *this was the real Rafe,* the man who interrupted her sleep, made her dream about things she oughtn't. Locked in his embrace, she buried her hands in his hair. How fine it was to hold this man in her arms—the smell of him, the taste of him, the way his muscles coiled beneath her hands.

"Come to my cabin," she whispered.

Rafe dropped his hands abruptly. "I can't, Maggie. I wish I could but I have to get Amos."

Burning with embarrassment, Maggie quickly backed away. "I understand. You have respon-sibilities. I…I don't know what I was thinking."

"Ah, Maggie, don't look like that. I would, if I

could. And don't say you don't know what you were thinking because I was thinking the same thing."

"Sure you were," Maggie said softly. *Story of my life*.

Chapter Eight

Judging from the sparse number of people attending the cabin clinic, Maggie guessed she was going to have to take her show on the road again. With only a few days left to dispense medical care, she took to the road the next morning, armed with a makeshift map Louisa had drawn for her. This time she headed north, the morning sun not yet a burning ball of August heat. She was glad of the opportunity to explore more of the countryside; this was her favorite part of her job. *As long as her tank was full*, she never minded the lonely hours on the road. As long as her tank was full, she laughed to herself, remembering her ill-fated arrival in Primrose.

Driving the narrow roads of the White Mountains, she was pleased to find that Louisa's directions were pretty good, because she found the first family on her list with no trouble. Word having got around about her presence in town, she was cordially received and invited to examine the children. When she noticed that the mom was pregnant, she offered to check her out, but the woman refused. Having given birth to her other children at home, without incident, she was reluctant to get involved with doctors. Didn't she have three pretty girls to vouch for that? Sending a smile their way, Maggie agreed. But she made a mental note to find out who the local midwife was.

Her second appointment was nearby, and so was her third, but her fourth visit proved more difficult to locate. Two wrong turns took her an hour out of her way, at which point the sun was high noon, and the heat was deadly. A nearby mountain stream was the answer to her headache. Spotting a public access sign that promised trout fishing, Maggie climbed from her van with relief. Grabbing her sandwich and thermos, she scrambled down the hill to the edge of the narrow river. Shucking her sandals, she eased her toes into the cold water and sighed happily. Splashing herself till she felt human again, she then returned to the shore. Leaning against a tree, she opened her sandwich and thought, *this was as good as it gets*. She was still thinking that an hour later as she dozed, when someone whispered in her ear.

"Doc, you awake?"

Opening her eyes, she saw Rafe Burnside squatting beside her.

"I am, now. How did you find me?"

"It was easy enough. I stopped by Louisa's and she told me your schedule. What are you doing up here alone? Aren't you afraid of bears?"

"Bears?" Maggie said uncertainly.

"And bobcats. You really might want to be careful where you nap."

"Thanks for the advice." She shuddered. "I guess I got sleepy... Someone mentioned there was a natural inroad this side of the mountain, good for a small ski slope. I was going to investigate, but the heat got to me."

"You've been talking to Jim Ransom," Rafe said, clearly disapproving. "He's been hawking that idea for years. He likes to think his little plot of land is the next Stowe Mountain. He hasn't got a lick of sense, so beware."

"Beware of what?" Rafe had so many rules.

"Beware of a selfish man who may only be in it for the money."

"Isn't everybody?" Maggie sighed, not impressed with his argument.

"There's more to improving Primrose than building a ski slope, much less a farmer's market. Thinking things over, I don't have any real objection to the market, but preserving the mountain is more important than a ski slope. The mountain provides for us as long as we respect it. Over half a dozen small farmers work this mountain. You know how many ski slopes there are between here and Maine? A hundred? Two hundred? Who knows! Do we really need another when you can practically walk to the next one? I've told that to Jim a thousand times but apparently he doesn't care to listen, if he's still pitching that idea."

Maggie was unconvinced. "What difference would it make if there was another ski slope, if it helped Primrose?"

"But would it?" Rafe asked her patiently. "What about all the goods and services that would have to be brought in to accommodate such a deal?"

"But you don't mind the idea of a farmer's market?"

"You don't have to tear up a mountain to open a farmer's market. Just clear some land and set up a few tables."

"Rafe Burnside, you've been thinking!" Maggie laughed.

"I've come to think that it may make sense," Rafe said, blushing slightly. "Fannie's right, something's got to give, but a farmer's market is not the same as an overblown ski lodge and a motel— Oh, great! I can tell from your face that Jim didn't mention the part about a motel! A motel that would need access roads, a major septic system construct, new power lines, water lines—a whole slew of things that would not benefit the mountain. And what about the things the town would need to supply? Doctors, dentists, supermarkets… You paying me any attention, Maggie?"

"Point taken." She sighed. "No, Mr. Ransom did not mention anything about a ski lodge. I assumed it was a day tripper kind of thing."

"There's no such thing as a day tripper, these parts." Rafe smiled as he flicked her nose. "Once we get you, we never let go. You know, Doc, I didn't drive all the way up here to argue. We have unfinished business, remember?" he said, his eyes narrowing.

"We do?" Maggie frowned.

"We do." Brushing her hair from her forehead, Rafe pressed a light kiss to her brow. "Salty, but sweet."

"Oh!"

She watched as, with a slow, lazy smile, Rafe lay down beside her and stretched out his arms.

"Come here, Maggie," he said. "Come lay beside me."

A request easily filled. Sliding down to lie beside Rafe, Maggie nestled into his embrace and rested her head on his shoulder, her curls a delicate red fan against his golden-brown skin. They lay together for a while, talking quietly, aimlessly, surrendering to the hazy summer heat. Her eyes closed in dreamy contentment, Maggie almost didn't notice when Rafe began to nuzzle her neck.

His touch light, his hand explored her bare shoulder, crept down her blouse to outline the pillowy circle of her breast. Maggie firmed instantly at his touch, her breasts swelling, wanting more, wanting him to touch them…taste them. She could no longer pretend she had any desire to stop him, if she ever really had. *Oh, yes, touch me*, she sighed on a cloud of desire.

Rafe must have read her thoughts because, one by one, he unbuttoned her shirt until she could feel a cool breeze on her bare skin. "Layer upon layer," he said and smiled as he eyed her lacy camisole with great interest. Lowering his head, he pressed his cheek to her hidden breast, and smiled when he felt Maggie shudder.

"So responsive," he murmured, smiling into her eyes. "I think I could get to like blue silk very much." His teasing touch made her arch into his arms.

"Yes," he whispered. "I want you, too. See how much I want you?" Holding her hand, he drew it down to his groin, coaxing her to feel the swelling bulge beneath his zipper.

He was large, he was hard. Maggie shivered with anticipation. He wanted her as much as she wanted him. She could feel her own wet warmth, was intensely aware of her physical response to Rafe, the almost unbearable anticipation that rippled through her body as it readied for him. And it seemed he was just as ready for her.

Finding the zipper clasp, Maggie slowly drew it down and spread her hand across the bare skin she had exposed. His heat against her palm was dulcet, but the black hair crinkling beneath her fingers drew her hand in another direction. Her nails skimming the cotton of his boxers, she forced her way beneath the elastic band and slowly traveled down his belly.

The head of his penis was hard and dotted with moisture. Yes, he, too, was ready.

"Stop, Maggie! Don't!" Rafe whispered, pulling away from her abruptly. "I'd be less than worthless, if you did that anymore." He smiled crookedly.

Rising, Rafe threw off his T-shirt and pulled off his jeans. Reaching down, he unclasped Maggie's belt and slid her own jeans down, then covered her body with his. Wrapping her legs around his waist, he felt her wriggle into position until her body blended with his. Understanding her need, he entered her slowly, allowing her to adjust for his size. She was so moist, though, it only took a moment.

It was almost too fast. Rafe had to still himself in order not to come, then and there. But nestled in her body, he could not avoid the sensation that he was home. Opening his eyes, he caught her chin gently. *Thank you,* he thought, as he kissed her tenderly, and hoped she could read that message in his eyes. Her dreamy smile telling him she did, he began to move, her beautiful body taunting torment, her flesh against his unbearable.

"If you keep moving like that, Maggie—" Rafe was barely able to speak for the blood pounding through his veins "—we'll have to do this all over again."

"Yes—" she laughed unsteadily "—all over again."

Then the world spun and together they shattered into a million pieces. Wave after wave overcame them until they collapsed in a heap on their soft bed of leaves. And in the middle of nowhere, on the edge of a ghostly mountain, Maggie found herself falling in love.

She must have dozed off because the next thing she knew, Maggie found herself waking to a cool hand cupping her cheek. Instinctively, she leaned into its gentle fold, but the hand slid away to slip beneath her neck and raise her mouth to his. They made love again. The next time they slept, it was deeper.

Later, much later, when they were dozing in the shade, her leg draped across his, her fingers making sworls of dulcet the dark hair on his chest, Maggie wondered what they were doing. But she was reluctant to question Rafe too closely. There wasn't anything to ask him anyway, she told herself. She would be leaving soon, even if she did—*finally*—believe in love at first sight.

Maggie's budding relationship with Rafe was of some concern to her, because she had been having second thoughts about leaving. Whatever happened between them, she didn't want it to affect her decision. And the more Maggie thought about setting up a private practice, the more she knew it was the right thing to do, but she still sought Louisa Haymaker's input. "I've been thinking of opening a private practice," she told Louisa over breakfast the next morning. "Yes, here in Primrose," she said to Louisa's inquiring look.

"Well, wouldn't that be wonderful for us!" Louisa

said, but surprised Maggie with her hesitation. "Still…to move here…Maggie, could you really handle the change? It can be pretty lonesome here in the dead of winter, let me tell you."

"That's why I've come to you for advice. You know what it's like to live in a small town. My not having a family, I expect my experience would be similar to yours. Except for one major difference. You were born here, everyone knows and loves you, and takes care of you, too."

"They do, you're right. These legs…" Louisa said, frowning at her swollen ankles. "Sometimes I can barely manage the stairs. But since you began treating me, it's made a world of difference. *You* take care of me, too, when you think about it. And everyone speaks very highly of you, Maggie, so you don't have to worry on that account."

"But tell me what you *think. Tell me what to do*," Maggie said, sounding whiny even to her own ears.

Louisa's probing eyes studied her curiously. "Are you all that unhappy back in Boston?"

The question gave Maggie pause. "I'm not *precisely* unhappy… But I *could* be happier. In the small things. Which become the big things, don't they?" She smiled weakly. "Like, I've always wanted a garden. And I thought it would be nice to own a house, instead of handing my money over to a landlord in exchange for a one-bedroom walk up. If I had a house, I would have room to stretch, too. I've always wanted to oil paint, too, but I never had room for an easel. And someone gave me a pottery wheel a few years back, but I have no room to set *that* sort of thing up! And—"

Louisa smiled good humouredly. "Maybe you know what you want to do without my telling you."

Maggie smiled sheepishly. "Maybe I do."

"Maybe you just want a little encouragement."

"Maybe I do."

"Well, child, you have my vote!" Louisa laughed.

The first chance she had, Maggie drove over to Bloomville and searched out their new hospital. Introducing herself to that particular medical community seemed the logical thing to do, to be sure she'd be welcome, not be stepping on anyone's toes. Entering the sleek, new three-story building, the first thing that struck her was the warmth and cheerfulness of the gaily painted lobby. The cream-colored walls were decorated with the requisite impressionistic prints, and the harsh lines of the vestibule were softened by tall ficus trees. But the best was the children's corner. Bounded by three bean bag chairs, it was a softly carpeted unit made up of neatly shelved toys and games. It even contained a small library arranged to occupy older children. The entire staff seemed pleasant and receptive. It was a bit of a change for Maggie, more accustomed to the frenetic pace of Boston Mercy Hospital.

Stopping at the information desk to introduce herself, Maggie was greeted warmly. When she explained her mission, a doctor, overhearing her request as he checked charts, offered to take her on a quick tour before he headed for lunch.

"I'm Peter Messer," he said extending his hand to Maggie. "These ladies here can vouch that I give the best hospital tour in the building. Come on, girls," he said when the nurses giggled, "vouch for me! I have a feeling we're looking at…ahem…fresh blood, here. Her visitor's pass says she's a doctor."

The head nurse smiled at Maggie and nodded her agreement. "But watch out, he's a joker, big time!"

"Thank you for those kind words, Amy!" Dr. Messer said. "Dr. Tremont, I'm going off duty in a few minutes. If you care to wait, I never tire of showing this place off."

"Of course I'll wait," Maggie said, "and be glad of it! I was hoping that someone would have time to spare me a tour, but I didn't really think it would happen. I was really expecting to just walk around and maybe ask a few questions. Your free time is my good luck."

Ten minutes later, they were on their way. Knowing the hospital would be her liaison in an emergency, Maggie asked so many questions that Peter's short tour lasted over an hour. Its facility was state-of-the-art, its staff young and energetic, and as importantly, backed by a mentoring program of retired doctors. Who could ask for more, Messer wanted to know.

"It's a great hospital, except for the food," he laughed as he finally led Maggie to the cafeteria. "It's not the worst, of course," he promised as they stood in line to fill their plates, "but I've been working to upgrade the menu. It's been an uphill battle, though. They keep insisting there's been no call for tofu burgers," Peter confided as they searched for an empty table, "but my friends tell me otherwise. Do you think someone's pulling my leg?"

Maggie suspected it was both, but didn't like to say so, she just quietly followed his lead to a table.

Doctor Peter Messer was a tall, scruffy-looking man in his mid thirties with a shock of light brown hair in desperate need of a trim. When he told her he was an orthopedic surgeon, Maggie almost fell off her chair.

"Oh, so you're one of those people who think a surgeon should wear a suit and tie." He grinned when he saw her glance at his T-shirt. It was kelly-green, had a picture of a man riding a dragon, and the word *Aquaman* printed in bold above the graphic. "Hey, the kids love it!" he assured Maggie with a laugh. "To be honest, a lot of people agreed with you when I arrived here, but they've gotten used to my ways, and my nails are *always* clean. See?" he laughed again, something he did a lot, Maggie noticed, as he spread his hands across the table.

They *were* clean, immaculately manicured long fingers that did look like they belonged in an operating room.

"Okay, I'm convinced." Maggie laughed. He was such a gentle man, his camaraderie was so infectious, she knew they could become fast friends.

"Good," Peter said, stirring his coffee. "When I went to my first interview here, I managed to borrow a sports jacket, but I think it was my credentials that sold them. That and my barbecue sauce. I light up the charcoals every Sunday, in case you're interested. If you came this weekend, you could meet some of the staff and townsfolk, feel out the situation some more. And have some of the best grilled burgers in New Hampshire."

"Thank you for the offer."

"Sure thing. Besides, it's always a good idea to have a pretty woman at a party," he said, his brown eyes teasing. "But to tell you the truth, Maggie," Peter said, growing serious, "it's also partly selfish. If you're asking me if you'll be competition, I have to tell you that there couldn't be enough medical care in this neck of the woods. When word reached Bloomville about the van missing its Primrose stopover last April, we tried to get a team together to make up the deficit, but not enough doctors could find the time, that's how busy we are. I may be a surgeon, but I pitch in working the night shift twice a week, and that's a lot of overtime, as you probably know. I schedule my surgery accordingly because if I didn't help out, it would put a worse burden on others. Another doctor around here would help us immeasurably, so when you ask if I'd be happy for you to join us—sweetheart, I'd be thrilled!"

"Wait, Peter," Maggie said. "I'm grateful for your support, but I was thinking more along the lines of setting up my own office, in Primrose."

Peter was stunned. "Are you serious, Maggie? You'd be so isolated. Hey, don't get me wrong," he said, when he saw her face fall. "Sure, the White Mountains are beautiful, but Primrose has the reputation of being so ecology-minded that it takes a town ordinance to cut down a tree. People say that Primrose doesn't have decent roads because they don't *want* decent roads. They don't want the extra traffic tourists would bring if Primrose became more accessible."

"So I've heard," she said, thinking of her conversations with Rafe.

"Have you spent any time there, Maggie? It really *is* Heartbreak Hotel."

"I *have* spent time there, not much, it's true, but I think I could handle it. I'm used to being alone, so I'd probably fit right in, and since I'm not married and have no kids, I don't have to worry on that account."

"Listen, sweetheart, I have no family either, but I do like a little companionship, once in a while. Maggie, you may think you're a loner, but in Boston, if you want some company, you call up a friend, meet them for dinner, take in a movie. In Primrose, you can forget about movies, and don't even mention the word *restaurant* there. You have to drive forty miles to get anything beyond a quart of milk—there to Bloomville, as a matter of fact. And you better like to read because their TV reception is less than perfect. If a cable guy shows up, they shoot to kill."

Maggie laughed. "The truth is, I *do* mostly read, but I appreciate your warning."

Peter shook his head good naturedly. "Okay, Maggie, have it your way, but do yourself a favor. *Don't* lease your space for more than a year!"

Chapter Nine

When Maggie called the Mobile Clinic's head office the next morning and ran the idea by her supervisor, he was less than enthusiastic. He was sure she would be a success, she was too good a doctor not to be, but had she really thought this out? She'd been with them for so long, was such an important member of the staff… Was she not being a little impetuous? Well, if that was the way she wanted it. They would take her back, of course, if she changed her mind. And of course, she would be missed.

But *who* would really miss her? Maggie wondered as she clicked shut her cell phone. In the early years, when she had first joined the staff, everyone had been terrific. Coming back to Boston after weeks on the road, the staff would get together, trade war stories over dinner. But since they all traveled so much, it was a hit-or-miss situation. Holidays were better because everyone tried to be home, but Maggie soon found those visits awkward. Suddenly, there were spouses to meet, babies to gush over. Dinner tables grew longer, more crowded, noisier. And no matter how much she tried, Maggie began to enjoy these affairs less. Perhaps if she'd had a husband to accompany her, or her own baby to show off, it would have been more fun.

What she *had* begun to do, the last few years, was to make excuses for declining invitations. Sometimes she would say she was already booked, going to so and so's for the holiday. One Christmas, as a change of pace, she bought herself a plane ticket to Delray Beach. It sounded so nice in the newspaper ad, warm and sunny. It was great until she found herself sitting on the beach surrounded by a hundred lively families who'd had the same idea. She ordered room service on Christmas eve…and flew home the very next day.

Sometimes she thought that *after* she got married and had her own home, she would make a better fit. But she never married. Then she thought she would buy a house *anyway*, but somehow, she never bought that house. More than that, she had never learned to cook, never entertained, didn't even own a full set of dishes. She blamed it on her nomadic life, but the truth was, she hadn't had a real home since her father died, and hadn't wanted one. The void her father's passing left had never been filled, and it was an ache that pushed itself to the forefront the past few years. Now that she had the opportunity to do something about her life, the idea took fast hold. More and more, she was becoming convinced that moving to Primrose was an opportunity that might not come again.

Hence her conversation with Louisa. Then, somehow, Fannie Congreve heard about her plan and called to say she thought it was a terrific idea and that she would support Maggie in any way she could. Immediately, Fannie's friend, Molly Bernardi, called to say that her mother's house, standing empty the past five years, would suit a doctor admirably, and was hers for the asking. Not only would it make for a lovely home, but there was plenty of space for an office, and it *was* right in the center of town. It just needed a *little* carpentry work... Okay, make that a *lot*. And maybe a paint job, too. But it was hers—rent free for one year!— if she decided to try and make a go of it.

Unable to resist, Maggie drove over to see the house. It was a ratty shell of a building with a large front porch that sat on a distinct tilt. The overgrown yard hadn't seen a lawn mower in a hundred years, the windows needed replacement—Molly was right, it *was* in desperate need of paint—and Maggie could only guess what the inside must look like. She fell in love with it at once.

Accepting Molly's offer that very day, Maggie

put the wheels in motion to make the break from Boston. She contracted a cleaning service from Bloomville to make the house habitable. Hearing of her decision, some of the handier members of Primrose offered to update her wiring, hang a few light fixtures, and level the porch. At the same time, a painting party was arranged. If she stayed beyond the year, she would worry about major renovations then. As long as she had hot water and a stove on which to cook, she could manage.

In between hiring contractors, Maggie took the opportunity to walk up and down Main Street, to get a handle on the town. It was depressing to see the amount of stores that were abandoned and walk the crumbling sidewalks. But she was hopeful. With a little planning, and a lot of sweat equity, Primrose could find its place on the map once again, if…

There were so many *ifs* that someone less optimistic might be daunted. Not Maggie. The few stores that were operating were necessities. The pharmacy, which doubled as post office, was the busiest place on the street. But where the notions store was boarded up, its cracked wooden sign dangling from a chain, Maggie saw the possibility of a crafts center and sewing school. When she peered in an abandoned dry goods store, she saw a bakery. And when she came to the end of the street, she wondered if the town square might not be the perfect site for Fannie's farmer's market.

Rafe's enthusiasm was less pronounced, but that came as no surprise. Maggie had just sat down to make plans and organize her lists when he came knocking on her cabin door, a few days after she had met with Peter Messer.

"I hear tell you're planning to set up a practice here in Primrose."

"Well, hello to you, too," Maggie said, with a wry smile as he squeezed past her into the cabin.

"Sorry…hi…is it true?" Rafe demanded in a single stream of words.

"Okay, yes, it's true," Maggie said, quietly placing her pen on the desk. "I've been thinking along these lines a while and—"

Rafe cut her off. "You aren't doing this for me, are you?"

"For you?" Maggie repeated, puzzled. "How do you mean?"

"You know…you and me…" Rafe scowled.

"Granted you *are* an added attraction," Maggie admitted. "But you're not the whole picture, not even half. Maybe I'm feeling my age, but I think it's time for me to settle down, live in a house, maybe even plant a garden," she mused.

"And what would you know about gardening?" Rafe asked impatiently.

Thanks for the vote of confidence!

"Not a thing—" she smiled "—so I guess I won't start with lettuce."

"And what if things don't work out?"

Maggie took a deep breath. If Rafe was in the mood to be argumentative, there was nothing she could do about it. "Then I move back to Boston."

"I meant *us*."

"Is there an *us?* We've never discussed it."

"I— Yes, well, maybe you're right, but—"

"Look, honest to God, Rafe, I was talking to Louisa about setting up a private practice and somehow Fannie heard and called to encourage me. Then Molly Bernardi called to offer me her mother's house. Then a doctor from Bloomville Hospital volunteered to help me set up an office. I hate to sound like Fannie but it all seemed so…karmic. So I called my office to see how much leave time I had, and it turned out I could go on sabbatical, if I wanted. So I rented the Bernardi house, with an option to buy, if I like how things go."

"I don't believe it."

"Excuse me?" She frowned, her voice becoming chilly. "I told you a while back that I'd been thinking of doing just this."

"I thought it was…a conversation…in passing."

"Well, surprise, surprise. I like it here, so much so that I decided to stay. And if you think this isn't scary for me, let me tell you that my stomach is in a complete knot. But the way I figure, it's now or never. I've been drifting for too many years. It's time for me to think about *me*. And what I think is, my future is now, and it seems to be here in Primrose. My decision has *nothing* to do with you. There is no *us*, remember?"

"Come on, Maggie you know damned well that after what happened last week, *something* is going on between us. *Us. We.* I don't give a damn what you call it, I think I should have some say in this matter.

All I want is for people not talk about me. I want whatever we do to be private."

"In a small town?" Maggie asked, incredulous at his naïveté. "*Perhaps* we could be discreet about the sex part, although I doubt it, but *not* the part about seeing each other."

"I don't want to *hide* anything," Rafe protested. "What happened the other day between us was great. *Everything* that's happened between us has been great. I haven't felt this way about a woman in years. But I would hate it if people started asking me questions, and that's exactly what would happen if anyone knew I was seeing you. When Rose left me, people kept asking me about her for ages. *Why did she leave...where did she go...was she coming back...* Like I knew, for chrissakes! *Which I did not* because she didn't have the decency to tell me she was leaving, much less leave a damned forwarding address! The questions got so bad, I stopped going to town."

Collapsing on a chair, Rafe slumped down and stared at Maggie, exhausted and confused, and hoping she would have an explanation he could live with.

Maggie stared back, wondering how to approach him, then cut through his silence with a silken thread of words.

"People talk, Rafe," she said softly. "It's human nature. People are curious, and you're right, they can be downright nosey, but nothing you do is going to stop them. It's all in the way you handle it. From what I've heard—yes, even I have heard the stories—you didn't handle Rose leaving very well. It seems that you became an out and out recluse after she left. Why? Did you think folk were going to laugh at you, think less of you? Rafe, Primrose loves you! They would never do anything to hurt you. But you apparently don't believe that, the way you turned your back on your friends."

"I didn't turn my back. I was upset. Coming home one day to find Rose gone—*literally*—the house empty, her belongings gone, a note on the kitchen table telling me where my son was… Why is my reaction so hard to understand?"

Maggie nodded. "The kind of man you are, I can understand all that, but for *seven years,* Rafe? *Seven years?* Louisa says you've become a hermit."

Rafe hesitated. "I guess it got to be a habit, but there was no joy in coming down the mountain after Rose left."

"What about Amos? Wasn't he reason enough?"

"I never did know what to do about him. Not that I didn't get plenty of offers of help. There were a whole flock of women who were dying to cook for me, clean the house, do the laundry… It might seem generous to you, but to me it was a choke hold. I just wanted to be left alone. It was easier to take Amos into the orchard with me than complicate my life with another woman."

"Well, far be it for me…"

But her words didn't register with Rafe. Watching him, bewildered and so obviously unsure what he wanted, Maggie's heart went out to him. But like a thousand country love songs that mourned true love, she knew she was at the end of an affair that had hardly begun. Well, so be it. But she *would* have her home.

"Look, Rafe, I won't deny that I have feelings for you. The attraction is very, very strong. But you're right, we moved way too fast. And I have to be honest, Rafe, if I have to choose between you or having a home, the home is going to win. So, maybe I should concentrate on that for a while. I won't say I didn't know what I was doing when I slept with you, and I won't say it wasn't wonderful because it was, but the kaleidoscope has shifted. The last couple of weeks have shown me that I'm needed here. What with Louisa encouraging me to set up an office, Fannie asking me to help her get her market going, Molly's offer of her mother's house…" Maggie shrugged. "It all seems to be falling into place, don't you think? Everything but you…" she said quietly, her eyes unflinching. "But that's okay. Nothing's perfect."

Rafe leaped to his feet, his eyes stormy. "Did you just throw me out of your life?"

His angry accusation made Maggie pale, but she was determined to stand her ground. "The door was always open."

"Damn it, Maggie, this is not why I came here, and not what I wanted to happen."

"Oh, I think it's *exactly* what you came to say," she said, lifting her chin. "We probably should have had this conversation *before*…not after. I can't imagine how I allowed the lapse," she said bleakly. "Even if the attraction was strong… But what the heck, Rafe, I just did you a big favor. Now you can go back to your apple orchard and not have to worry about some strange woman upsetting your apple cart."

"Maggie, stop! I'm not the monster you're making me out to be. I take care of what's important. Amos…Louisa… Anyone who needs a helping hand knows where to find me."

"Just nobody get too close, huh?"

"Until you," Rafe nodded. "You caught me unawares."

"And now you don't know what to do."

Rafe looked at her hopefully. "You do understand."

"All too well, but not enough to earn you any Brownie points. It's my job to help people confront their problems, not run away from them."

"I'm not running!" Rafe protested.

Maggie flushed, but kept her composure. "If I practiced deception of any kind, I would be of no service to the town whose doors I want to open."

"And this doesn't include cutting me some slack?"

"Come on, Rafe, it's not a matter of cutting you slack. No need to do that for a man I was halfway to loving. You caught me unawares, too." She smiled painfully. "But I'm not the kind that loves blindly, and you won't be the first guy things didn't work out with."

"This seems pretty easy for you." Rafe glowered.

Unconsciously, Maggie crossed her arms over her chest, and shook her head regretfully. "You won't hurt me that way, Rafe."

"Then what *do* you want?"

Maggie's smile was shadowed by her inner pain. "When we first met, I joked about going to Cinderella's ball, but, Rafe, there was a reason I never went to that silly dance. I never needed a Prince Charming. I was always on the lookout for a man who could take care of *himself,* not *me.* I do fine on my own, thank you very much. I want someone to help make my house a home, not a castle. I thought it might be you, but who the hell was I to make such an assumption. Just because we…we… You have a lot of thinking to do before you can go there with any woman. Rafe, you embrace your memories so fiercely that you have no room for anything else, much less a romance. Rose, or the memory of Rose, is still more important to you than what I or anyone else could do for you. Sorry, Rafe, but I can't compete with a ghost."

Rafe looked as if Maggie had slapped him. He began to speak but he couldn't manage a word, his throat was so tight.

"Go on, Rafe, go on home. We never quite got off the ground, so what's the difference how it ends?"

True, Maggie's plans had probably come as a surprise to him, but no more so than to her. And the part about her feelings for him had been real, and she had a hunch they were true for him, too. She guessed that was part of his panic. No doubt the news of her settling in Primrose had been too threatening. They probably nearly gave him a heart attack, she thought with a brittle laugh. No grace under fire, here. Well, she was *not* going to let this affect her plans. But her stomach roiled as he closed the door behind him.

Chapter Ten

While the cleaning service from Bloomville ripped apart the Bernardi house, and the town put together a painting party, Maggie drove back to Boston to do the paperwork required by her office to place her on sabbatical, and to give up her apartment. She didn't reach Boston until evening, but it was nice to drive through the city at dusk, pass Faneuil Hall and wax nostalgic over the crowded sidewalks. Not that she was going to change her mind about moving to Primrose, but city bred as she was, crowded sidewalks had their allure. And when she walked through the door of her apartment, and felt the chill of disuse curl around her shoulders, she knew she was doing the right thing. The clutter of

an apartment hardly used and dusty from neglect
was a story in itself. She hadn't realized how cut off
she was until she read her isolation on the bare walls,
in an empty fridge, and the silence of her message
machine.

It took a nearby Chinese restaurant less than half
an hour to deliver some hot food. In that time,
Maggie turned the air conditioner up, took a cool
shower, slipped into fresh pajamas, and collapsed in
front of the television. Tomorrow would be soon
enough to take inventory of her possessions, what
she was going to ship to Primrose, what she was
going to donate to the Salvation Army, what things
she could transport in her car. She had to smile when
she realized that she would have to give the shipping
company very precise directions to Primrose, maybe
even draw them a map if she ever wanted to see her
things again. But it seemed fitting that if she were
going to drag Primrose into the twentieth century, it
should start with a Fed Ex delivery.

The next morning, she drove over to the office of
the Mobile Clinic of New England to process her
leave, to return their van, and say her good byes. The
process was so rote, it didn't take very long. Her
most difficult chore was heading over to Boston
Mercy Hospital to discuss handing her small practice
over to another doctor, not a big issue because she
had already spoken with the director. That done, she
took the elevator to the fifth floor where she kept an
office. It might be small, but she did have a few
things she would like to keep—pictures her younger

patients had drawn for her, thank you cards from others.

Her tiny office was a shabby affair that she had never bothered to decorate. Still, she thought she would never see the color of mustard again without recalling the dusty, tiny room where she had spent so many hours poring over her patients' charts, where she had memorized the dreary view of the gray courtyard from her uncurtained window as she determined plans of treatments, mourned the death of her first patient. *Get shut of this, girlfriend!* she told herself. *You're not the sentimental type, and never were! Get those damned boxes filled and be on your way!*

So that's precisely what Maggie did for the next two hours, until her office was empty and she was ready to haul her belongings to her car. It was good therapy, too. Maggie was amazed at how calm she felt when she was done, everything neatly taped and labeled. If she had to be honest, the old gray building that had been her workplace for so many years had been the site of very few memories beyond the dramatis personae of her patients. *That* she would miss, of course, and was hopeful she would soon have new ones to replace them. But all in all, she was glad to leave the hospital quickly and quietly, notwithstanding the years she had been there. She might have a change of heart if she delayed, the whole shift of her life was so daunting.

Luckily, there weren't many people to bid good bye. Most of her friends were on vacation, so she was surprised to see one of her best buddies, as she made her fourth trip to the car. Wheeling herself down the hall in a wheelchair, her left leg in a cast, Jody Caraway greeted Maggie with a cry of surprise.

"Maggie, is that you?"

"Jody?"

"Where on earth have you been?"

"In New Hampshire."

"When did you get back, and why haven't you called me? I thought…we all thought… Honestly, no one knew what to think! I even went to the director and he told me you were fine, said you were in New Hampshire, but— Maggie, why didn't you answer your cell?"

"I'm sorry you were worried. My service was a sometime thing. It's true, though, I've been hiding out in a small town in the White Mountains. But what about *you?* What happened to *you?*" Maggie asked, pointing to Jody's cast.

Jody's cheeks turned scarlet. "It's too embarrassing to say. I tripped about three weeks ago—right after you left, come to think of it—while I was on duty, in ER."

Maggie smiled sympathetically. "I suppose if you have to break a leg, that's the place to be."

"I guess. I got great care," Jody admitted, "after they stopped laughing."

"Stopped laughing?" Maggie repeated, shocked.

"I suppose it *was* pretty funny. And to give them their due, they didn't know how seriously I was hurt. It was lunch time, I was in a hurry, and came face-to-face with a food cart. Unfortunately for me, the food cart won."

"So I see. Poor baby."

"It gets worse." Jody grinned. "The dessert of the day was strawberry Jell-O. Very red stuff. Sort of the color of my face, when I finished sliding all over it and came to full stop—*on my butt!* They had to operate and insert a pin to stabilize the bone. So here I am, on sabbatical for three months, but what the hey. They offered to put me behind the admitting desk. *Me*, an OR nurse! It was a nice offer, but I had so much sick time that I declined. I come in now, one or two days a week, but just to volunteer in the library. Keeps me sane. I had no idea that staying home could be so boring."

"If you had married Matthew Danforth way back when, you would have had a husband, and probably a few little Danforths to distract you."

"That's why I didn't marry him!" Jody laughed. "Hell, Maggie, I'm not the motherly type, you know that. My career is my life, and I like it that way. When Matt married Penny last winter, it was almost a relief, I felt so guilty turning him down. And look, nine months later, she has twins! I couldn't be happier for them, *and me*."

Maggie followed her friend as Jody began wheeling herself down the hall to the elevator.

"What about you?" Jody asked, glancing at the box Maggie was holding. "Why do I think there's a story in that box?"

Maggie laughed. "It would take too long to tell

you. Can I interest you in some dinner? We could talk, then. My treat."

"Your treat? Then definitely." Jody grinned. "I'm sure I can fit you into my busy schedule. When?"

"Now, if you're hungry."

"When am I not? I'll follow you."

"You're driving?"

"For sure. It's my left leg that broke, not my right. I have crutches in my trunk, which I'm supposed to be using, but I only got them this morning."

"Well, then, follow me. I have lots to tell you!"

Half an hour later, Maggie and Jody were sitting in the Athenian Diner, waiting for their burger specials while Maggie filled Jody in on all the gory details of her summer. Jody was so intrigued she didn't say a word until Maggie was done, then leaned back and smiled. "Wow. Some people have all the fun."

"It's had its moments." Maggie sighed. She had been careful not to say too much about Rafe. It wouldn't translate well. Bad love affairs were best left to gather dust on a high shelf.

"So, when can I join you?"

"Where?" Maggie asked, confused. "I'm leaving in a few days."

"In Primrose, silly! You did say you needed help, and let's face it, I'm not doing anything important for the next three months. Like I said, I'm bored stiff, and this smacks of an adventure. Now that you have that big house…" Observing Maggie's look of surprise, Jody backed off. "It was just a thought…"

Maggie reached across the table and squeezed

Jody's hand. "Are you kidding? I would be thrilled if I had a friend with me, and if it were you, that would be the best part. But are *you* serious, Jody? It's pretty primitive, and I'm not only talking about the house."

But Jody was resolved. "If there's running hot water, I'll be fine."

"Hot water, yes." Maggie grinned. "But no pizza parlor."

"Now *that* is serious… I suppose I *can* bring my own supply of pepperoni, but it won't be the same." Jody frowned, but Maggie saw the teasing light in her friend's eyes.

"I was intending to plant some basil."

"Okay, you're on." Jody grinned. "I have some loose ends to tie up, but look for me in a week, maybe less. That is, if I can find your small town."

Maggie, too, had a few loose ends to tie up. She spent the next few days running back and forth to Fed Ex, to the Salvation Army to whom she donated a great many things, met with her landlord, canceled her utilities, and said good bye to her neighbors. Before she knew it, she was back on the road, her car crammed, her heart beating faster, and Jody following closely behind.

The evening she arrived back in Primrose, she had the oddest sensation that she was home. When she pulled up in front of her formerly shabby, rundown house, she was smiling. And astonished. The entire building had been transformed. The peeling walls had been scraped and painted pale yellow, the trim had been redone in white, and a new red door greeted her as she stepped from her car. And although it was patchy and badly in need of seed, the lawn had been mowed, the rubble cleared.

"Cute," Jody said as she hobbled up to her friend's side.

"You have no idea," Maggie murmured.

It was the same inside. The house had been painted white, top to bottom, the cleaning service had scoured the place, and the light switches actually worked. It wasn't a renovation, but it was a start, and judging from the amount of work accomplished in one week, Maggie knew she had the whole town to thank.

"I'm impressed," Jody told her as she walked around the first floor, her crutches tapping staccato on the shiny wood floors.

"Me, too. You have no idea what I left behind. Someone—*many someones*—have performed a minor miracle, here."

"It's very pretty," Jody agreed. "Or it will be when it's furnished."

"Don't you worry, Caraway. Shopping is high on my list."

Seeing how drawn and pale Jody had become since the drive, Maggie forbade her friend to unpack. "How about we put you to bed? The guest room is upstairs, second door to the right. The beds are the one thing I told the cleaning service not to throw out. There will be plenty of time to unload the cars in the morning."

Exhausted, Jody offered no argument. Together, they climbed the steps to the second floor. "I can't wait to shop," Jody said wryly, testing the mattress. "But you can be sure I won't feel any broken springs tonight," she promised, as she stretched out.

Jody's leg *had* been paining her, and though she was not one to complain, Maggie could see the strain around her eyes. "Go to sleep, Jody. We'll talk in the morning," she said as she headed for the door. "You need to meet Primrose with a full head of steam. Believe me, I've gone the other route and it doesn't quite work," she added, recalling her inauspicious entry into the town. "And hey, Jody… thanks for coming."

Imperative that certain medicines be refrigerated, Maggie was sorting her vials when she heard a car pull up. Hearing a door slam, she hurried to the front parlor to see Rafe walking up the newly mown path. Surprised, she opened the door before he could knock.

"Rafe! I didn't expect to see you tonight."

"Should I go?" he asked, clutching his hat nervously.

"Don't be silly." She smiled. "I don't need to make an enemy before I've even unpacked my bags. We were both too upset, the last time we spoke. To be honest, I hated us parting like that. Come in, please. I was just sorting some stuff but I'm really too tired to do much more."

Maggie stepped aside as Rafe walked into her new home. "Well, you said you were going to do it, and you really did," he said looking around the newly painted house.

"More like the town did, and a fantastic job, too," she said proudly.

"I smell soap," he said as he passed her. "I heard from Louisa that you had hired a cleaning service from the other side of the mountain. Painted, too. I heard that practically the whole town helped."

"That's what I heard, too. They did a wonderful job, don't you think?" Maggie asked as she led him into the sparsely furnished living room.

"I do. I never would have thought this place was salvageable."

"Surprised, huh? Me too!" She laughed merrily. "How is Louisa?"

"Oh, she's fine. She's Louisa. She can hardly stop talking about your coming to live here. Everyone is, even Amos."

"I know. She wanted me to stay at the motel, but I wanted my own house. That was the whole purpose. How is Amos?"

"He's fine. He's up at the Congreves'. Frank and I are taking the boys camping in the morning."

"How nice. Then shouldn't you be in bed?" Maggie asked.

"I was delivering Louisa some last-minute supplies and she mentioned you were returning today. When I saw your light on, I thought you might be able to use some help."

"Good timing. I was about to call it quits, but I'm not averse to taking advantage of free muscle power.

There's some heavy stuff in the trunk that I was too tired to deal with. Once I loaded up in Boston, I was too excited to sleep, so I just got in the car and drove. But I'm paying for it, now. I'm exhausted."

"Impulsive, as ever." He smiled as she led him to her car. "Whose car is the other?"

"That's my friend Jody's car. She wanted an adventure and said I fit the bill, so she's offered to help me out for a few months while she recuperates from an accident. Her leg's in a cast."

"How can she help if her leg's in a cast?"

"You don't know Jody."

Judging from the shadow in Rafe's eyes, Maggie guessed he wasn't pleased by the arrival of her friend. "What?"

"Nothing."

"Come on, Rafe. What's wrong?"

"It's just that… A few months? She's a generous friend."

Maggie nodded. "Ah, yes, I see. Another stranger arrives in Primrose. Encroaching civilization. Your worst nightmare, huh? Well, if it's any consolation, she's only staying till Thanksgiving."

Just like you, she could almost hear him thinking as she followed him out into the cool summer night.

Between the two of them, Maggie and Ráfe had both cars completely unloaded in under an hour. The empty rooms took on the semblance of a warehouse, the way they piled things haphazardly, for Maggie was too tired to organize. The last box in hand, Maggie took a moment to gaze up into the dark sky, a black velvet canopy that looked near enough to touch, the night air a sweet-smelling balm to her tired body. "It's never so dark in Boston," she said quietly.

"Going to miss it?" Rafe asked, following her gaze.

"Boston? A little," Maggie admitted.

Rafe's look of disbelief was so pronounced that Maggie had to laugh. "Yes, well, okay, *a lot,* but not enough to change my mind," she warned him. "My next order of business is furniture. I—"

"Maggie, I'm sorry."

Startled by Rafe's unexpected turn, Maggie was uneasy. She hoped he wasn't going to bring up the past on the very night she was beginning her future! Whatever happened between them had been so brief, a candle flicker, it didn't even seem worth the breath to blow it out.

"I'm a fool, I know, but I— Last time we spoke— okay, *argued*—I guess I panicked. Maggie, are you listening?"

"I'm listening," she sighed. "Of course I am, but do we have to talk about it? I have no problem leaving things the way they are. I would prefer it, actually."

"But I was out of line."

"You wouldn't be the first."

"Come on, Maggie. I'm trying to apologize."

Maggie pursed her lips. "I understand that, but I'm not sure that an apology is in order. You went with your feelings. There's nothing wrong with that."

"That's it?"

"What more do you want?"

"I've been doing some thinking while you were gone." Rafe took a deep breath. "I *do* want us to go somewhere, Maggie."

"Really?" Maggie smiled, trying to tamp down her sarcasm. "Well, I've been thinking, too, and this is what *I* think, Rafe. I have just made an enormous commitment to this town and don't want to spoil it with a sour affair that didn't last longer than a minute."

Rafe paled. "A minute can be a long time. I was hoping that maybe we could get back on track."

Gazing up at the stars, Maggie was silent, searching for words. "We were never *on track*, as you put it," she said quietly. "We were in lust."

"Oh, come on, Maggie, it was a little more than that!"

"Rafe, I handle life and death situations for a living—which may account for my crushing honesty." She smiled ruefully. "Neither inclines me to mince words, so you'll forgive me if my patience wears thin. On the other hand, people always know where I stand. That said, the way I see it, for one wonderful afternoon, *if* we were going somewhere, we got stalled at the gate. But I *am* glad you stopped by," she said, determined to end the conversation on a lighter note. "Your help was appreciated, I promise."

"But not my presence," Rafe snapped.

"Rafe!" Maggie protested. "I would never feel that way about you. Look, we were headed in a certain direction it turned out you weren't sure you wanted to go. Well, you gave me pause, too. Now that I've decided to live here, I'm grateful. It would have been very uncomfortable for me to try and establish my authority, and be marked at the same time as Rafe's cast-off. How about we back up a bit, start with the part about friendship, and see how that goes? I have a hunch we're both weak in that area."

"My feelings for you are stronger than that."

"Perhaps they are, and I won't say I'd object to exploring that…um…facet of our relationship somewhere down the line. But right now, I think a little breathing time is in order. Now that I've rented this house and I'm staying awhile, we'll have plenty of time to sort things out."

"I suppose you think it's selfish of me to pester you like this, the first night you arrive in Primrose."

"You're not pestering me."

"But I'm not much of a welcoming committee, am I?" Rafe insisted.

Maggie smiled. "When you think about it, you're the same one I had when I first arrived in Primrose. I don't mind consistency…"

And as she watched Rafe climb into his truck, his long, lean body moving with an elegance few men owned, Maggie thought, *Hey, cowboy, don't think that sending you away wasn't the hardest thing I had to do today.* It had taken all her willpower not to throw herself into his arms. But she had her dignity to maintain. She had her pride.

Once burnt, twice shy.

Chapter Eleven

Maggie woke the next morning to the sweet sound of birds chirping in the tall oak tree right outside her bedroom window. It made her smile, and she had a feeling it was going to be that kind of day. The only sad note was her rift with Rafe, but it couldn't be helped, and she decided not to dwell on it. She didn't want anything to spoil her return to Primrose. Sliding her feet into her slippers, she made her way to the shower and turned on the spigot full blast. She admired the fresh paint job and made a mental note to check out some wallpaper patterns. Towels too, something summery and cheerful. She wanted a cheerful house, and by golly, she would have one.

Jody was all ears as she listened to Maggie's

decorating ideas an hour later while Maggie scrambled them up some eggs. Looking round the bare walls, Jody smiled as she stirred her second cup of coffee. "Just think. One day this place will be filled with more junk than you'll ever need. But I have to admit that waking up this morning to rustling leaves was a nice change from the traffic that blasts me awake in Boston. When I've just come off the night shift, and the bus route runs right beneath my bedroom window, rush hour can be pretty raucous. This decision is definitely right for you. I can see it on your face. I think maybe I'll be visiting a lot."

Maggie was so happy at Jody's freely given words, she burst into tears. "Don't worry," she said, with a sniffley giggle. "It's just the changes and all."

"Well, you did a complete about-face with your life." Jody smiled as she handed her friend a tissue. "I think I would worry if you *didn't* lose it. Hey, you know what? Let's take our mugs out onto your fancy new front porch. That way I can put my feet up— well, one of them, anyway—and watch the grass grow while you cry."

Poring over a map of New Hampshire while they finished their coffee, Maggie and Jody decided to head for Lancaster and do some major shopping. "But on the way, I want to stop and say hello to someone—someone I want you to meet."

Jody smiled. "I just *knew* there was a man connected to this, somehow."

Maggie shook her head. "Guess again. Louisa Haymaker is very much a lady, and the broad back upon which much of the renaissance of Primrose rests."

"I thought you said it was that guy whatshisname, Raymond."

"Rafe Burnside," Maggie corrected her, trying to remember what she'd told Jody. "The town loves and respects Rafe, and if he objected to anything, I'm not sure they would buck his authority. He denies he has any, of course, but he does, so I tread carefully around him. But it's Louisa Haymaker who is their dowager queen. She lords it over the town, and loves every minute of it, too. Oh, the town will do most of the work, don't get me wrong. She's eighty something, if she's a day. But she's the one who said to give it a go."

"But surely Mr. Burnside couldn't reject any good ideas that would revive a dying town."

"Jody, he's a good man, he really is, but he's so close to the earth that it's hard for him to see much value in anything else. He only supports the farmer's market because he's been made to see its connection to the land. It's the land he believes in, not the people. He has staked his whole life on the mountain. When it fails him, he thinks it's something *he* did. Not planted early enough, not fertilized correctly, didn't let the land lay fallow…"

"Wow, you *have* been in the country!" Jody teased.

Maggie shook her head. "Long enough to *spout,* but not long enough to really *know.* What I do know is that when the townsfolk expressed a wish to

spread its wings a little, he wasn't all that suppor-
tive, at first. He truly loves the White Mountains and
his great concern is to preserve them. Any idea that
threatens their ecology earns his disapproval. So,
when we talk about a farmer's market, his concern
is not the market *per se,* but how to manage the in-
creased traffic into Primrose, the problems tourists
generate, the gas pollution of additional cars. His list
is endless."

"And where do you come in?"

"I fell in love, first with the people, then with the
area. Oh, and I want to go on record as whole heart-
edly supporting the market."

"But to actually leave Boston, Maggie? Quit your
job? Leave your friends? There must be more to it
than that."

"I was ready, Jody. I've been ready for years, I
just didn't know how to make the changes I needed.
Restless, a little bored, a lot lonely. It hit me last
Christmas. Nothing specific, just a sense of dissatisfaction. The plain fact is, I never had a strong sense
of belonging, in Boston. Maybe once, but like I said,
not lately. I know I haven't had a real sense of family
since my father died, and that was so long ago, I'm
surprised it stayed with me, but it did. I want roots,
Jody, friends for my old age, a garden—"

"You? A garden?"

Maggie laughed. "Why does everyone say that to
me? Yes, I want a garden! It sounds silly, I know, I
can tell by your face, but I tell you, Jody, when I
stumbled into Primrose, something happened... It

was as if the town was waiting for me," she said thoughtfully.

"I don't think you're silly," Jody promised. "I've just never heard you speak like this before."

"That's what I mean." Maggie smiled.

"Well, it makes a certain kind of sense," Jody reassured her. "I recognize some of those feelings."

"And here you are, still ready to come along for the ride? And don't think I'm not grateful."

"And don't *you* think I'm not going to get something out of this for myself," Jody warned her with an impish grin, "even if I don't know what it is."

Maggie and Jody headed over to Louisa's right after breakfast, but it was that rare moment when the gas station sign read *Closed,* and Louisa was nowhere to be found. Leaving her a note, they headed for Lancaster, a city considerably larger than Bloomville, and boasting a large mall. They had some serious shopping to do.

The day was long and tiring, particularly for Jody, dragging her cast around the way she was, but they managed to order new beds and bedding, a few appliances—*Yes, you do need a dishwasher, Maggie!*—and even stopped at a poster store where Jody treated Maggie to some wall hangings.

When they got back to Primrose it was nearly midnight, so they headed straight for bed. Sleeping in, they decided to give themselves an easy day and took their breakfast out to the porch once again, to enjoy the summer weather. They were still munching the last of their toast when the Fed Ex truck arrived with Maggie's Boston delivery. Easy day, indeed! They soon found themselves staring at the boxes for two bookcases, two desks, and an examination table, and wondering how they were going to put it all together.

"There's something to be said for ready-made furniture," Jody teased.

"Yes, but the price of this pre-fab stuff can't be argued."

"Too true. So, what's the name of the local carpenter? Consider it a housewarming gift."

"Ask and ye shall receive. Somebody up there loves you!"

Startled to hear a male voice, both women jumped. They had been so busy emptying boxes that they didn't hear the front door bell. As one, they turned to find Peter Messer standing in the doorway, leaning on the doorjamb, his tawny head of curls as wild as ever, a wide grin on his puckish face.

"Hi, there, Doc. It's my day off, so I thought I'd come say hello. But I have a feeling that I'm going to work harder than I expected," he laughed, glancing at the upheaval.

"Peter!" Maggie cried, scrambling to her feet. "How nice to see you. I'm honored!"

"So honored that you're going let me open a few boxes, right? And you should see what I have in my truck. Gifts from the clinic—*used,* most of it—but the price is right. And extra supplies to get you through your first few weeks."

"For which I'm grateful. Jody, this is Dr. Peter Messer, from Bloomville Hospital. Peter, this is my friend Jody Caraway. Jody is the head ER nurse at Boston Mercy Hospital. She's come to lend me moral support while her leg heals."

"Yeah, I know, I'm too old for this sort of thing." Jody laughed when she saw Peter check out her cast.

"Uh, oh, I detect a story here." Peter smiled.

"A regular comedy show," Jody promised.

Jody listened, all ears, as Maggie and Peter bantered, but what she *saw* was far more interesting. A handsome doctor driving fifty miles or so, *to make small talk?* Make that a drop-dead gorgeous doctor! Well, Maggie *was* a sweetheart, and when she smiled, her gray eyes *did* sort of glow… Like now…

"Your timing is good. We were just about to try and make sense of the instructions in these boxes," Jody heard Maggie explain.

"And any and all volunteers are welcome." Jody grinned. "The reward for helping is dinner."

"Where's the toolbox?" Peter laughed. "I'd stay for a tuna sandwich. Just let me go get my electric screwdriver out of my trunk. But just so you're warned, it's never been opened. Come to think of it, it's never even made it out of the car."

"So how do you know the battery is charged?"

Peter paused to think about that. "I guess I don't! A bad sign, huh? But owning tools is part of being a homeowner, isn't it? And it *was* on sale."

"Better put Sears on your shopping list." Jody

smiled, as she watched Peter go find his toolbox. "Better yet, put Dr. Messer on your list!"

"On *your* list, maybe." Maggie grinned impudently.

"Okay, sure, and winner take all," Jody said, amused by the idea. "But he didn't drive all this way to see *me*."

Three hours later, amidst an uproar of laughter and mismanaged directions, the three amateur carpenters had completed two bookcases, and were working on a desk when Jody called it quits. "Sorry, folks, but this cast is so annoying, I'm exhausted. Anybody mind if I lay down for a while?"

Maggie was so embarrassed that she had not suggested it herself, she almost threw Jody out of the room. After shooing her friend out the door, she turned to the littered floor, hands on her hips. "Do you think this will ever become a doctor's office?" She sighed.

"Of course it will!"

But the littered floor did not reflect the optimism Peter felt. The truth was, he was every bit as awkward with tools as he had warned. So, when Rafe came knocking on the door minutes after Jody had gone off to nap, Maggie was glad of the sight of him. After their conversation of the other night, she hadn't been sure she would ever see him again, so she took his appearance as a positive thing. She could imagine how difficult it must have been for him to knock on the door. The smile she sent him as she opened the door was tremulous but determined. Almost as determined as his hesitant smile.

"Maggie?"

The smile she sent him as she opened the door was tremendous. "Hello, Rafe."

"I saw the boxes outside and wondered if you needed more muscle power. For friendship's sake," he added with a crooked smile.

Impulsively, Maggie gave him a hug. "That's how I greet my friends." She smiled into his surprised face. "Of course I'm glad to see you!"

"The other night…it was so… I just wanted to make sure you knew that I was glad you were moving here, Maggie." Peering past her shoulder, Rafe smiled at the yards and yards of packing bubble and crumpled brown paper that covered the newly waxed floor. "I see you already started. Is that mess really going to be a piece of furniture?" Spying Peter Messer perched in the middle of the confusion, Rafe's face took on a darker hue. His dismay was so obvious, Maggie had to bite back a smile.

"Please come in," she urged, motioning him inside. "Let me introduce you to my newest friend. I got lucky. He stopped by, too, to help me unpack."

Hearing their footsteps, Peter struggled to his feet, careful not to step on any pieces of wood.

"Hi. I'm Peter Messer." He smiled, as he extended his hand to Rafe. "Glad to make your acquaintance. And this is not a mess, it's a construction site, although I can see how you could make that mistake." He grinned. "But if you ever came into my surgery when I was operating, you would not say the same."

"You're a doctor?"

"An orthopedic surgeon over in Bloomville, and a better doctor than carpenter, I assure you, although I hope you never have to find out. And you are a carpenter, perhaps?" Peter asked hopefully, eyeing Rafe's dusty jeans were.

"Guess again," Rafe said brusquely.

"Rafe is a farmer," Maggie explained quickly. "He owns the Burnside Apple Orchard, about seven or eight miles up the mountain. A beautiful stretch of land with woods and a small pond."

"Really? I have a great recipe for apple pie. Your farm sounds like the place we ought to be right now. In the pond," Peter explained, as he wiped the sweat from his brow.

Rafe frowned at the awkward way Peter was holding the screwdriver. "You look like you need some help."

"Oh, no," Maggie interrupted, "I wouldn't dream of asking, especially after all the help you gave me the other night. We'll make do. I can see you don't have Amos. Are you on your way to pick him up?"

"Amos is visiting his grandma for a week or so. All his cousins visit her the end of every summer, just before school starts."

"Lucky kid," Peter said, as he picked up a sheet of instructions.

"So I could stay and help, if you wanted…"

Maggie shook her head. "No need. We're doing fine."

But Rafe was already squatting beside Peter.

Gently, he tugged the instruction sheet from Messer's hand. "Allow me."

Peter smiled. "If she won't, I will!"

Between them, they wrought such a miracle that even Jody was surprised when she returned two hours later.

"Wow! Doctor Tremont, I do believe you have an office!" she cried happily.

Looking proudly around the room, at the examination table tucked against the wall, the desks and bookcases, Maggie nodded. "It is going to happen, isn't it?"

"Looks to me like it already *is* happening. We've just got to find the iodine and we'll be in business. Ah, hello there," Jody said, spotting Rafe. "You must be Rafe. I'm Jody Caraway, Maggie's good friend, shopping partner and chef du jour. Which brings me to announce that the salad is on the table, and the spaghetti is almost ready."

"Spaghetti?"

"Spaghetti *and* a fresh tomato sauce. I got ambitious." Jody laughed. "A nap does that to me. So why don't you all go get washed up? You too, Rafe. You seem to have earned a meal, if this room is any indication."

Ten minutes later, the starving work crew sat down to dinner. After a second helping of spaghetti, Peter declared the meal was ample award. "Nurse Caraway—*Jody, darling*—I'd marry you first thing tomorrow, if you promised to cook me a meal like this every night."

Jody grinned as she watched Peter replenish

their wineglasses. "You're not too much of a male chauvinist!"

"Hey, I'd do the dishes!"

"Yeah, right. And what about the blood tests?"

"I have connections." Peter winked.

"Well," Jody said, her face studious. "I've always wanted to marry a rich doctor and sit back and enjoy life."

Maggie almost choked on her wine. "Oh, sure, right, like you even know how to spell the word *marry*. Don't let her kid you, Dr. Messer, she's already turned down *that* opportunity."

"Well, then, at least I don't have to worry about being married for my money. There isn't any at this end, anyway. Just a lot of student loans."

Rafe was skeptical. "Are you kidding? I thought all doctors were all rich."

"Well, you just met the exception, my friend. I have no plans to move to the big city and become a plastic surgeon—at least, not until the kids start college."

"Kids? I thought you were single."

"Sure, but down the line there might be a few kids, maybe six or seven. Maybe even a wife!"

Maggie laughed. "I think you just lost Jody, Doc."

"Women!" But the disgust in Peter's voice was belied by the twinkle in his eye, and won him a rare smile from Rafe. *Rafe smiling?* Maggie was shocked. Was it the wine? she wondered, because if she wasn't mistaken, Rafe was enjoying himself. An impression that was short-lived, when he pushed back his chair.

"I have an especially long day, tomorrow. I'm

driving over to Heron to see a man about a horse. It's a surprise for Amos. He's been begging me for years. Maybe it will save me on gas."

"You probably have to feed a horse just as much as you do a kid," Peter warned Rafe as they gathered up the dishes. "Most boys I know eat as much as a horse, or so my sister tells me. She's got three."

"You're absolutely right, if my son is any example." Rafe smiled as he helped Peter clear the table. "Ever been to a horse farm?"

"No, never. Is that an invitation?"

"If you have to work, I'll understand."

Peter rubbed his jaw, trying to hide his smile. "Rafe, your enthusiasm knocks me over. I have the late shift rotation tonight and usually head straight home to bed, but for *you* I will make an exception. I'm used to pulling all-nighters, anyway. I'll meet you at the farm, if it's not too far. I can sleep afterward. I assume the ladies are invited, as well?"

Rafe shrugged. He had known that forty miles was not going to discourage a country doctor, and he sort of liked Peter Messer, even if the poor fool didn't know his way around a hammer.

Peter wasn't a fool about *all* things, though. He knew Rafe hadn't dropped in accidentally. The way Rafe tracked Maggie's every move, the guy might as well post the banns. And honestly, coming straight from a twelve-hour shift, Peter didn't *really* need to visit a horse farm. But if Jody Caraway was going… Damned if that girl didn't have the cutest pair of twinkling blue eyes!

Chapter Twelve

The Heron Horse Farm was a series of immaculate barns surrounded by miles of white picket fence. The owner was a slight, wiry man named Mr. Fry, who greeted them warmly and proudly offered to show them around the grounds. They were enchanted. Rafe, almost as knowledgeable as Fry, stood by, a small smile playing on his lips while they asked Mr. Fry a million questions.

Rafe couldn't take his eyes from Maggie. Every question she asked, he was all ears, and as Mr. Fry led them around the barn, Rafe was all eyes as he trailed behind them. In those tight jeans, well, Maggie had this real nice way of moving her hips… When she climbed a fence to get a closer look at a horse Rafe was right up there with her, elbow to elbow. Charmed by her interest, he lost track of time as they discussed the merits of a young palomino Mr. Fry was urging Rafe to consider.

"He's beautiful," Maggie exclaimed.

"Yes, he's pretty nice, not a true palomino, of course—he's too red for that, more of a chestnut, or he would cost me the earth. But nice enough. And young enough for Amos to train."

Sharing a little bit of fence with Maggie as they watched the colt trot around the field, showing off, Rafe had to admit that Maggie had come to mean a great deal to him. She was exactly the kind of woman he had always imagined for himself. Well, all right, *not always*, not when he was younger. When he was younger, he had wanted only Rose— upside down, sideways, in bed or out, it didn't matter to him. It had been mostly about sex. And why not? He had been a young stud, and Rose had been more than willing, her own desire a match for his. They'd had fun, too, until things changed. Pregnant, she had been miserable. But he had never thought she would leave, *it never occurred to him she would leave*. People didn't do that, hereabouts. He should have paid more attention. Not only had she pulled up stakes, but she had left him with a small son to raise. *Well, thanks much for that, Rose,* he thought, as he stared absently at the palomino. Amos. The one bright spot in his dreary life because when Rose left, he had shriveled up and died, at least a part of him had. All the pleasure that remained in his life shrank to the size of Amos. A big burden for a little boy.

And then this scrawny, rain-soaked woman drives into Primrose on a godawful thunderous night, sneezing into a wad of dirty tissues—and his heart starts thumping like the Mad Hatter. A man ought to be warned. A man ought to know better, he thought, stealing a glance at Maggie's face, profiled so nicely by the sun. She sure wasn't sick now. On the contrary, she was brown as a berry, covered with freckles, and smelling sweet as a bouquet of wild roses. Hell, she had him wondering where the nearest hay loft was. Him, a grown man of forty!

And that Peter guy had better not be poaching on his territory, Rafe thought grimly. Not that Maggie was his to own, but that was how he felt, and he didn't want any nonsense from Messer. Because, even though they were worlds apart, Maggie had seen something in him worth having. And no matter what she said, if she'd seen it once, she might see it again.

"Rafe? Rafe? Why are you looking like that?"

Lost in his reveries, Rafe almost didn't hear the woman he was dreaming about. "How? How am I looking, Maggie?"

"Like you were thinking about something seriously upsetting."

Helping Maggie climb down from the fence, Rafe held her in his arms a heartbeat longer than he needed. "You've got it all wrong, Maggie. If there's one thing I'm not, it's upset. As a matter of fact, I'm pretty happy just to be standing here with you."

"Oh." Rafe's admission caught Maggie off guard. She collected herself just in time to see Jody hobble from the barn.

"Hey, Rafe," Jody called. "Mr. Fry said to tell you there's a horse in here you might want to look at."

Relieved to be interrupted, Maggie followed Rafe to the barn. "I guess I know one little boy who is going to be very happy." *Even if his father isn't.*

It was one o'clock before they headed home. Leaving Jody and Rafe to discuss the merits of miniature horses, Maggie walked Peter to his car.

"Listen, Doc," Peter said as he lowered his car window. "Do you think you and Jody could make it over to Bloomville next Sunday so I could show off my culinary skills?"

"I'd like that very much, and I'm sure Jody would, too."

"Good. My field of expertise is chili, so don't forget the beer. Bring Johnny Appleseed, too, if he's able to tear himself away from his trees."

"Peter, hush!" Maggie darted a quick look at Rafe as he stood talking with Jody in the shade of a leafy red maple.

"Yeah, yeah, I know." Peter grinned. "Salt of the earth, and all that. And go figure, I even like him. But you have to admit that smiling doesn't come easy to him."

"He hasn't had much to smile about."

"Oh, come on, Maggie, we all have our crosses to bear, but being in love shouldn't be one of them.

Yes, that's what I said. Rafe Burnside is in love, and it isn't with Jody! I don't think he knows what to make of Jody. Or me. Or maybe even you. But Jody and I don't count. By the way, you *do* know that he thinks I'm sweet on you," Peter said, his eyes dancing.

"No!"

"Yes! And hey, princess, he might have been right, if Ms. Caraway's baby blues hadn't stopped me dead in my tracks. But don't you dare let on to Jody."

"I did wonder, but my lips are sealed. She'll be a tough nut to crack, though."

"Well, seeing as how I don't know where I want us to go, I'm not going to worry about that, now. I'd just like to have a little fun and she looks like the type to enjoy a good laugh. But she did catch my eye, right off, so I won't deny the chemistry is there."

"And on that note…"

"*And on that note,*" Peter said, revving his engine, "just so you know, I will endeavor to make Sir Galahad as jealous as possible."

"It's going to cost you in gas," she grinned. "*And just so you know,* I won't cooperate."

"Come on, Maggie, don't you want to liven Mr. Burnside's life up a bit, give him something to angst about? It's good for the soul…cleansing."

"Peter, you are outrageous!"

"That I am! And it's hard work, too! Now, come give us a little peck on the cheek. That should be enough to give yonder knight a heart attack."

"And you a doctor!"

"The kind of palpitations Rafe would get are very healthy." Reaching for Maggie's hand, Peter pressed a smarmy kiss to her palm.

"Oh, you wicked man!" she laughed as she pulled her hand away.

"Don't look, but I think I got him where it hurts already! Bye, Jody! So long, Rafe," he shouted as he drove away, leaving a trail of laughter and dust behind him.

Maggie watched Peter leave, then strolled over to Jody and Rafe, careful not to meet Rafe's eyes. But she was keenly aware of his displeasure as she took the seat beside him in the truck. Hunched on the seat, she tried for nonchalant.

"That guy's a real joker, isn't he?" Rafe muttered.

"I think he's pretty funny, myself," Jody piped up.

"But you'd think a doctor would have more…I don't know…more dignity."

"Maybe he saves it for the operating room," Jody suggested.

"So, you agree he's a joker."

"On the contrary," she protested. "I think he's a great guy, and generous. Look how he helped Maggie the other day, on his day off, no less. And coming out here to join us after pulling an all-nighter at the hospital. If he likes to fool around, is that a crime? Doctors are under a lot of pressure. Patients want so much from them. As for surgeons… you can double that quotient. One mistake, just one little mistake, can be disastrous. Clowning around is probably a tension breaker for Peter."

"I suppose," Rafe said, surprised at how Jody had jumped to Peter's defense. "I never thought about it like that. You're talking about yourself, too, aren't you, Jody?

"I guess," Jody admitted. "As head nurse of the emergency room of Boston Mercy Hospital, I promise you, it's no place you want to be on a Saturday night, Rafe."

Maggie and Jody worked hard the next few days setting up the rest of Maggie's office. When all the boxes were opened, the supplies sorted and arranged, they rewarded themselves with Peter Messer's offer of lunch. A quick call and it was all arranged, all except for Rafe who said he was too busy to play. But when they set out on Sunday morning, he was waiting by the curb.

Bloomville was a small bustling town that Maggie had not seen close up, so she took advantage of Jody's curiosity to drag them around the town. Main Street was five blocks long and lined with cutesy boutiques disguised faux Victorian, half a dozen restaurants, and a small lakeside hotel that sported water skiing and a man-made beach. The thriving town made her wonder how Primrose got lost between the cracks and she voiced her concern to Rafe, who heard the question with a strained look.

"They have the people, they have the resources." Walking down the cobblestone street, a shadow crossed his eyes. "Of course, it depends on what you're after, doesn't it?"

"I suppose. But how bad could it be?" she asked, watching a family of tourists exit a store, their arms laden with packages. "It seems good for the town. You hate it, don't you?" she said, when she saw Rafe pull a face.

"I don't hate it. I'm here, aren't I? I just wouldn't want to live here."

"Too big? Too noisy?"

"I'm a farmer, Maggie. This bustling about is...I don't know how to explain it... It seems sort of superficial."

"Score one for blunt speaking." Maggie smiled.

"But this *is* your idea of a good time," he said flatly.

"Hmm, yes, it is," Maggie said thoughtfully. "It's not my *only* idea of a good time, but yes, once in a while, I do like walking down a busy street surrounded by lots of people, buying frivolous things I don't really need, maybe treating myself to an ice cream cone."

"Chocolate," Jody chimed in.

"With sprinkles."

"Lead on." Jody giggled. "We'll bring some to Peter's."

Rafe said nothing as he followed the two women down Main Street. Entering the local ice cream parlor, he listened as they held a serious discussion about the merits of chocolate fudge versus vanilla praline versus black raspberry velvet. Unable to decide, they bought a pint of each, and threw in pistachio—*just for good measure*, they laughed. Armed with dessert, they headed over to Peter's.

"Hey, glad you guys could make it," he greeted them as they shuffled through the door.

"Glad to be here," Jody said, as she hobbled over the threshold.

"Dessert," Maggie said, smiling as she handed him the ice cream.

"Smells good." Rafe nodded as he followed the women inside.

Peter's tiny house was cluttered but welcoming, reflecting his easygoing personality. A huge blue sofa dominated the L-shaped living room, along with assorted stuffed armchairs and a coffee table. A slate of thick gray carpet covered the floor, and family pictures and photographs decorated two walls. But the centerpiece of the living room was his display of ceramic bowls and figurines that lined the deep window ledge. It seemed that Peter collected pottery, and he was not reluctant to show it off. The pieces he had were so elegant, and of such high quality that Maggie asked if he could take her to visit some of the local studios.

Peter's house was a home that reflected his joy of life, and, to Rafe's mind, made more apparent the barrenness of his own. So he was doubly depressed when he sat down to lunch, to fresh made chili surrounded by so many condiments, he didn't know all their names. A fresh baguette, an urn of butter, a huge green salad—everything so simple, but tasteful. And some really terrific beer, *imported from Brooklyn*, Maggie laughed, for she had made the selection. Listening to the chatter at the table, the friendly banter so alien to him, Rafe was even more demoralized, but he roused himself to join in. To smile, at the very least. Well, to smile faintly, in any case. A smile made more difficult to sustain as he listened to their conversation, when it veered at one point to shop talk.

Even in his moodiness, Rafe was intrigued by the medical fraternity to which the others belonged, although his viewpoint was that of the patient. He had a momentary twinge of anger at what Primrose was missing, *what the children of Primrose were missing,* so damned dependent on the state to send a lousy van. He felt guilty that he hadn't organized a trip to Bloomville to get the kids their for shots and stuff. Why, he wondered, had they all been so passive when the van missed them, last April? And not that Primrose could ever hope for a hospital of its own, but hell, they didn't even have a town physician, much less a clinic! How could he have ever thought to discourage Maggie from settling in Primrose, when she was possibly the best thing that had happened to the town in years?

And worse, something that had been bothering him lately, what part did *he* play in the neglect of the little town? Was Maggie right when she said that he'd been so bent on licking his wounds that he'd lost sight of the bigger picture? Had all his fine talk about preserving nature only been a foil to hide away in the mountains? A way to keep a tight rein on Amos, the son he loved so much, who even now was beginning to strain at the bit? He knew that the people of Primrose looked to him for guidance, but the more Maggie brought things to the forefront, the more he felt he had somehow failed them. And all the ice cream in the world could not sweeten his pain.

"Wow, these are terrific, Peter. Homemade shortbread? They go great with the ice cream, don't they, Maggie?"

"All four flavors," Peter winked. "Did you leave any ice cream for the next customers?"

"I don't think that was a big problem." Jody laughed. "Listen, Messer, these shortbread cookies are terrific. You're going to make someone a great wife."

"Hey, I have an idea," Maggie exclaimed. "Primrose is thinking of starting a farmer's market, Peter, and these would sell like hotcakes. Wrapped in red gingham, tied with a pretty ribbon, a little note attached that said '*Baked by Dr. Peter Messer— From An Original Family Recipe.*' I know I'd be first on that line."

Peter laughed as he sipped his coffee. "Flattery will get you everywhere, ladies, but to be honest, I know how to cook three things, and you just ate two of them."

Rafe rose to his feet, annoyed and uncomfortable. He was beginning to see what Maggie meant, that he had stunted himself, hiding away the last seven years. Hell, he didn't even know how to joke with people, anymore. If he ever had, it was a skill long lost. "Look, would it be okay if we left soon? I think I see a storm on the way," he said, glancing out the window at the gray clouds that were gathering.

Twenty minutes later, Peter's guests were heading out of town. Tired from the long day and good food, Jody was already dozing and Maggie was pleasantly sleepy. Rafe looked at Maggie's drooping eyelids and pulled a face. "I guess it's a good thing the radio is working."

"I'm all talked out, anyway," Maggie said with a smile.

Then, before she knew it, she was being shaken awake.

"Come on, Maggie, wake up. We're home. Jody is already in the house, and it's beginning to rain. Come on, sleepyhead," she heard Rafe whisper, "we're home," so close she could feel his warm breath fan her cheek. Startled, she opened her eyes to find him staring down at her. "Jody is already in the house and it's starting to rain."

Slowly, Rafe lowered his mouth and brushed her lips with his.

"Rafe," she said softly, "this is not part of our plan."

"*Plan?* Do we have a *plan?*"

"Yes, we have a plan…to be *friends.*"

"Well, consider this friendly persuasion!" He smiled.

"What happened to last week?"

"Every time I think about that, I feel like a fool. You are becoming a learning lesson for me. I keep asking myself why I should hide my feelings."

"You said you were afraid to get hurt."

"I suppose, and I won't say I haven't been, but should it prevent me from a second chance?"

"Your opinion, not mine."

"Misguided. And you're not Rose."

"No, I'm not Rose. But I have no promises to make."

"I didn't ask for any."

"Just friends, then."

"Just friends…"

Taking hold of her hand, Rafe helped Maggie from the truck and flung his jacket over her head to protect her from the rain. Walking that way, tucked beneath his arm, his scent filling her senses, his heat burning her flesh, was maybe the most sensual thing Maggie thought she had ever done. Together they climbed the porch steps. Mesmerized, Maggie was a prisoner to the moment, watching as Rafe lifted a stray curl from her forehead.

"The first time we met it was raining. I remember the way you looked that night, standing on the porch, looking like a street urchin the way your hair covered your face. Your nose red, sneezing loud enough to wake the devil, shaking like a leaf. But courageous, the way you stormed into Louisa's looking—no, *demanding*—shelter. I figured you had just had one helluva drive if that was where you landed. You were quite a puzzle to me."

"I was pretty sick, and definitely beyond good manners. But as to puzzles, I'm the easiest puzzle you'll ever have to solve, Rafe. I have no secrets and I don't play games."

"Neither do I."

Maggie sighed heavily. "Then why do I feel like

you are? One minute you're cold, and the next you're hot."

Rafe's sigh was a study in frustration. "Maybe I don't know the rules—the rules that have to do with caring for someone."

"Oh, no, Rafe," Maggie protested impatiently. "You know how to care for people. Look what a beautiful child you have. Anyone seeing you together appreciates the deep connection. And the first night I met you, you were delivering food to an old woman in the middle of a thunderstorm. If that isn't caring, I'd like to know what is!"

Rafe's face was somber, his voice firm as he grudgingly accepted her compliment. "Thanks, but that isn't what I meant. I was talking about caring for *you.*"

Indignant, Maggie opened her front door. "My dear Mr. Burnside, I don't need caring for, and I don't want to be cared for. I'm not a child, I'm a doctor! *I do the caring!*" The door she closed gently was a loud sound, to his ears.

Rafe sighed all the way home. This was all *so* difficult for him! Just the sort of thing he hated. Why did women always make things so difficult? He wasn't a difficult man, was he? His thoughts glanced on Rose. There was a perfect example! He had only asked of Rose what a husband deserved: a home, a family, a hot meal after a long day in the fields, a warm bed. It had been the bargain they'd made. He'd kept to his part, so why then had she changed it? Why hadn't she told him how unhappy she was?

Pulling up to his house, Rafe shut the engine, but could not bring himself to move. Is *that* what had happened to Rose? Had the long hours he'd spent in the orchards, tending his fruit trees left her too lonely? Had there been too many empty hours in her day? Had she balked at a future that seemed hopeless and bleak? Looking back, he could see that it might have seemed so, to a young girl barely out of her teens. Looking back, he could see that having a young baby might not make up the deficit of an absentee husband.

And here he was now, tangling with Maggie Burnside, confused by expectations he had no idea how to meet. Damned if he wasn't even sure what they were! He never claimed to be more than an old-fashioned guy, and to his mind that meant providing a roof over his wife's head, and food on the table. But Maggie was right, she could do that herself.

Hell, he *told* her he didn't know the rules!

But if he didn't figure this out, he would lose Maggie, and what a fool he'd be to let her slip away. She was so interesting, and funny, and cute in a freckled sort of way. She had a great body, too, he reminded himself, flushing at the memory of their steamy interlude. Deeply, he regretted the gift of friendly banter, wished he had a more easygoing nature, was more affable, like Peter Messer.

Peter Messer. Definitely a threat. Competition of the worst kind. Handsome, likeable, interesting, charming… To compete against Messer, what chance did *he* have? The guy not only knew how to talk pretty, he was a professional—*a doctor*—one of her own. What chance did *he* stand, a dirt farmer from the boondocks? He could hardly remember the last book he'd read, didn't know squat about movies or plays or music, was basically uncultured. What did he have to offer a sophisticated city girl like Maggie Tremont? Jesus, with competition like Messer, should he even try to win Maggie over? And the worst was, judging from Messer's behavior, he didn't even care that much about Maggie. Okay, so maybe Rafe couldn't be *entirely* sure of that, but the way Peter joked around with Maggie and Jody, it *seemed* to be true. Certainly the man didn't love her the way Rafe did.

Love her?

Rafe slumped over the wheel, burying his face in his arms. What a fine mess he was in.

Chapter Thirteen

Gone Camping.

Fannie thought it ought to be a neon sign emblazoned on the heavens. But she settled for fact, the fact that Frank had taken the kids off her hands for a late summer adventure, bless him. That meant that she was free the next few days, or as free as the twins would allow. But it was enough, for it gave her the rare opportunity to visit with friends without the entire brood tagging along. So she hurried down to Maggie's as soon as the wheels of Frank's truck were out of sight. Finally Fannie had a woman friend who could help her to accomplish things that Frank could not.

Knowing Maggie had established office hours,

Fannie pushed the stroller up the path to the door that said *Doctor's Office*. She was greeted by an unfamiliar face sitting behind a shiny new desk, a set of crutches leaning on the wall behind her. Everything was new, not only the desk but the lamps, the chairs, the table and even the magazines on the table. Maggie had even filled a shelf with informational brochures regarding child care, various diseases, inoculation and the like.

"Hi," Jody said, greeting Fannie and her babies warmly. "Can I help you? Are you an emergency? If you're looking for Dr. Tremont, she's in with a patient."

"No, I'm not an emergency, I just look like one," Fannie laughed. "I'm Fannie Congreve, a good friend of Maggie's."

"Oh! I've heard all about you, Mrs. Congreve. I'm Jody Caraway, another one of Maggie's good friends. I see you've got your arms full," she said with a sunny glance at the twins. "Sorry I can't help you," she apologized, indicating her cast, "but if you want to join me in the kitchen, I was just about to put on a pot of coffee."

"No need to ask me twice." Fannie smiled, hoping the double stroller would fit trough the narrow halls. "This place looks terrific. Clean, too. I'm totally jealous."

"Jealous?" Jody asked as she fetched her crutches.

"You know what it's like to live with six men? There's *always* something on the floor to trip over, there's *always* a dirty dish in the kitchen sink, and the laundry alone could make a body sob!"

Jody laughed. "The laundry room is a place I studiously avoid. I drop my wash off at a Laundromat—thinking of which, that's *another* thing Primrose could use."

"A Laundromat is the least of it." Fannie smiled ironically.

"Laundry? Did someone just say laundry?" Maggie called as she came down the hall. "Fannie, is that you? And my favorite babies?" She smiled as she knelt to tickle the boys. "Teething, hmm?"

"Teething with a vengeance. Hi, Maggie, or should I say *Doctor Tremont*, since that's the hat you're wearing," she said, glancing at Maggie's white lab coat.

"Only two patients today, so far. Maybe I should get an inoculation program going. At least I'd get to see the kids."

"Try to be patient," Fannie counseled her friend. "No pun intended. I would imagine it takes time to start a practice."

"*Years,*" Jody agreed as she put up the coffee. "So that gives you plenty of time to sit down and join us, Maggie."

"Thanks. So what's up, ladies? Any good gossip?"

"Keep that up," Fannie twitted Maggie, "and you're going to fit Primrose like a glove!"

There wasn't much to gossip about, but there was much to discuss regarding the main topic of conversation in Primrose: the creation of the farmer's market. It seemed that Fannie and her friends had finally come to some conclusions as to the where, when, why and how. The *what* was still a variable, but Fannie and her friends were making phone calls to everyone—farmers and cheese makers and crafts persons—to please consider joining the market. They had been so successful that the first market was scheduled to open the first Saturday in October. "That will give us some time to get past the opening of school, and to advertise, and all. And not accidentally, it coincides with the beginning of the harvest."

"Is it September already?" Jody sighed.

"You betcha. With five boys, I count the days till school opens. Sometimes *the hours*," Fannie amended. "There's only one fly in the ointment, and that's partly why I'm here. Rafe Burnside—or rather, Rafe Burnside's apples. That stubborn man! He refuses to contribute to the farmer's market, and everyone knows he's got the best apple orchard in New Hampshire!"

"Does he say why?" Maggie asked, trying to assuage her friend's irritation.

"Not directly. I can't get a straight answer from him. He *says* he's too busy. *Then* he says he's got to pick them. *Then* he says he has to ship them. *Then* he says he has to press them. *Then* he says— As if everybody else doesn't have a thousand and one other things to do. I simply do not understand why he doesn't see the importance of this!"

"Maybe something else is bothering him," Jody suggested.

"Humph. Maybe it doesn't matter!" Fannie snorted

in disgust. "Don't get me wrong, I love Rafe, but this is bigger than just one person. This is as big as the town."

"Apparently he doesn't see it that way."

"*Apparently*. He says we have his blessing, but he doesn't have time to help. Well, *that's* no blessing, and so I told him. It takes a lot to make me mad, but believe me, I'm on the verge. Well, I *tried* to be angry, but that's hard to do with Rafe. He can be pretty scary when his dander is up, and when it's not, he has this look in his eyes that reminds you of a puppy that's been kicked one too many times. But I do own to wanting to shake him," she admitted dryly as she put one of the twins to her breast. "I would have, too, if he wasn't so tall. I even tried to sweet talk him, but that didn't work. That's partly why I'm here. It's your turn, Maggie. You go talk to him. If anyone can sweet talk the man, *it's you*."

"Oh, boy, have you got that wrong!"

"Why is that?" Jody asked, and when Maggie blushed, she smiled. "Ooh, Fannie, what have we here? Hidden depths?"

"Not as hidden as they'd like," Fannie said wryly.

"*And that*," sighed Maggie, "is the problem in a nutshell. Okay, yes, I admit it. Rafe and I did have something going—for the space of one whole minute! And then the poor fool panicked. He said that he hated having people know his business, especially if his business was *us*. So he quit me, plain and simple."

Jody and Fannie were appalled.

"Then he had the gall to tell me that he changed his mind! Just like that!" she said, snapping her fingers. "As if my feelings were of no consequence. Like I was a rubber ball."

"Oh, my!"

"I said *thanks, but no thanks!*"

"Of course," her friends murmured, exchanging cautious looks.

"And if either of you *dares* breathe a word about this outside these four walls, *I'll never speak to either of you again!*"

"Not a word," her best friends promised. "But…"

"No buts! And I'll bet the bank that's the reason he won't help you out, Fannie. Then he'd have to see me, and talk to me and make nice, and be wondering all the time if anyone was watching…talking about us… I'm betting that it's easier for him to not take part. It's just a guess, of course, but an educated one."

Jody and Fannie both fell quiet to the moment, each lost in thought.

"If you two dare to play matchmakers…" Maggie's voice held an unspoken threat, but the faces they turned to her were innocent.

Jody: *"Moi?"*

Fannie: *"Moi?"*

"Yes, both of you!" Maggie warned them sternly. "You both have that *look*."

"Come on, Maggie," Fannie reasoned. "You don't really buy that story that seeing you would be an invasion of his privacy. I sure don't."

"I agree—" Jody nodded "—and I don't even know the guy."

"Some men are lazy, you know, about this sort of thing," Fannie said thoughtfully. "After all, it takes time and energy to have an affair."

"An affair?" Maggie cried. "I can't have an *affair!* I can't just sashay into Primrose and start behaving like that, not in my position!"

"No, no, of course not," Fannie soothed her. "I just meant— No, you're right, of course you can't. But it isn't about an affair, anyway. Not for Rafe. Rafe doesn't do affairs, either. More likely, it's about becoming friends with a woman, another person even, given his lousy track record. Come on, Maggie, don't come down on me like that. I've known Rafe all my life so I think I can speak with *some* authority."

"She may have something there, Maggie. When we went to lunch at Peter Messer's, he seemed quiet, but I figured I didn't really know him, maybe he was shy. Was I wrong?"

Confused, Maggie started to pace the kitchen. "I don't know. I just know I fell for the man, and he seemed to do likewise. And then, just like that, he backed off. When I called him on it, he waffled. Then he wanted to be friends. Then he retreated. That man doesn't know what he wants!"

Jody laughed. "Sounds like love to me."

"Listen," Fannie said, matter-of-factly, "Labor Day is this coming Monday and some of us have organized a group cleanup of the town square, over where the farmer's market is going to be. It can't be utilized the shape it's in, it's so overgrown with weeds and all, so a crowd of us are going to fix it up, work out the table spots, that kind of stuff. Everyone is very excited. And in case you didn't know, Jody, this is partly Maggie's doing. Since she came to Primrose, we've all gotten energized."

"Why am I not surprised…"

"My husband, Frank, is going to mow with some of the other guys, and the kids are going to rake. We're even hoping to level a parking area. I'm thinking that if we got Rafe to attend, maybe something would give."

Maggie shook her head. "Sorry, Fannie, but if you want Rafe there, you'll have to find someone else to invite him. You, or Frank, maybe."

Fannie brightened. "Okay, Frank will ask him. That's even better. Rafe wouldn't refuse Frank."

Maggie nodded her agreement. "Just don't look to me for any involvement out of the ordinary, okay? I'm referring to Rafe, of course. He's not the only one gun shy."

Labor Day dawned bright and sunny, with the kind of crisp, cool air that hinted at autumn and roasted chestnuts. Maggie and Jody rose with the light, full of energy and excited, and anxious to arrive at the town square as early as possible.

"You know," Jody said as she climbed into Maggie's car, her cast leg stretched out before her. "I could get used to this life, country living."

"Well, real estate is real cheap in these parts." Maggie grinned.

"So I've heard."

"But I'm wondering if you might want to live closer to Bloomville."

Jody couldn't help laughing. "If you're trying to be subtle, Peter and I are not serious. *We're just looking.*"

"You may be *just looking*, but I don't think Peter Messer window shops. Not that he'd jump into anything blindly, but if he's looking, he's looking. You know what I mean?"

Jody's eyes filled with concern. "You know how I feel about commitment, Maggie."

"Does Peter know?"

"I've touched on the topic but I'm not sure what he's heard."

"Then you'd best make sure."

"I can't help what he doesn't hear," Jody protested.

"I know you would not encourage him..." Maggie hesitated.

"Of course not! But I like him. Very much."

Maggie sighed. "Jody, you can't have it both ways. If you're bent on remaining single, you have to make that clear to Peter."

"Do you think I should return to Boston?"

"That's not what I'm saying. I love having you here, and you can stay as long as you like. Just be careful, okay? You're both too nice to get hurt unnecessarily."

"Golly gee, you sound just like my mother!"

"Must be the doctor in me." Maggie grinned.

Just before they left, Maggie and Jody had brewed as much coffee as they could carry, so when they arrived at the town square, their thermoses were still hot. Many of the town had arrived early, also, and were already scattered about in a loose confederation of labor. Even Fannie and Frank had arrived, no mean feat, Maggie knew, with five boys to dress. Fannie was in the middle of setting up a long table, piling it with fresh fruit and a bowl of hard boiled eggs, when she spotted Maggie and Jody.

"Over here!" She waved, greeting them both with a quick kiss. The twins, bundled in blankets, were fast asleep in a nearby playpen. Louisa, too, had arrived early, bearing half a dozen freshly baked loaves of bread. Thus the coffee set up evolved into a breakfast table. But the biggest surprise was Rafe, unloading Louisa's bread from his pickup.

"Hello, Maggie."

"Rafe." She nodded.

Disappointed, but not surprised, by Maggie's chilly greeting, Rafe backed away. "Jody," he said quietly, as he settled the bread on the table. "I'd like you to meet my son, Amos."

Jody was thrilled. "I finally get to meet the famous Amos I've heard so much about! Hmm," she said, giving Amos a squint-eyed look. "You don't look like a cookie…but you do look sweet!"

Maggie rolled her eyes. "Amos, don't listen to

Jody unless you like goofy people. If you do, though, then you're in luck."

Jody grimaced, and beckoned Amos over to the table. "Want to help, famous Amos?" she whispered. "We could use some *real* muscle power here."

Pleased by her request, Amos scampered over to the other side of the table. Left alone with Rafe, Maggie found she had nothing to say. If the fleeting thought surfaced that this was how she often dealt with men—halfhearted attempts to manufacture short-lived relationships—she dismissed it before it took shape. She breathed easier when Rafe excused himself to go help the others.

Rafe had so keenly felt Maggie's rebuff that he sought the safety net of hard labor. Humiliated by her brusque greeting, he backed away, literally and figuratively. It was the only way he knew to handle his unhappiness. A good, honest sweat was the quickest way to mind-numbing exhaustion. Crossing the square, he joined the small group discussing the best way to approach the cleanup. At least *they* were glad to see him, he told himself, not daring to peek over his shoulder and see if Maggie was watching.

Which she was not, but she had *excellent* peripheral vision. She was able to watch from the corner of her eye as Rafe was greeted warmly by his neighbors. Back slapped, hand clasped, why, he was even smiling, shaking his head, probably teasing them about their thankless task. What, she wondered, had made him come? Fannie probably had got Frank to do some arm twisting to get Rafe here. Just look at him, now, climbing up onto that tractor, revving it up, looking far too good in his red flannel shirt, and those jeans that had seen so many washings that they'd shrunk to…just the right fit. Pulling his battered hat low across his brow, chewing on a slender reed of grass, palming the tractor wheel with his strong hands…

"Daydreaming, Doc?" Fannie asked as she set down a pitcher of iced tea.

Blushing furiously, Maggie turned her attention back to the table. "Just wondering."

"About?"

"About Rafe."

"So, the wind still blows that way, hmm?"

"That's not what I meant."

"No? Okay, whatever you say," Fannie said agreeably.

"I was only wondering how you got him here," Maggie insisted.

"It was Frank."

"I thought so."

"It wasn't too hard. Rafe almost always does what Frank wants, maybe because Frank is smart enough not to push him. And then, his curiosity probably got the better of him. Oh, and my secret weapon— Amos!" Fannie let on triumphantly. "There was no way that child was going to be left behind once my boys told him what was happening today."

"I think they call that dirty pool," Maggie scolded her friend.

"Yeah, I think you're right," Fannie agreed, distinctly unrepentant. "But he *is* here, and looking good, too, don't you think?" she declared, as she caught sight of Rafe.

Maggie's eyes narrowed as she watched Rafe maneuver the tractor around the far end of the square. "Oh, he's okay…" All right, so he *did* look good, but she *hated* that he did!

"Who's here?" Louisa asked, as she set a bundle of napkins on the table.

"Peter Messer, that's who!" Jody chuckled as she waved to the young man getting out of his car.

All the women turned as Peter ambled up to the table. "Hey, ladies, I heard you folk were having a barn raising. I didn't think you'd turn down some honest help. And I heard a rumor about food being served." Dramatically, he sniffed the air. "I smell coffee—Colombian, with a hint of French Roast."

"And there's fresh bread and hard-boiled eggs to go with it, young man," Louisa said, handing him a cup. "But every slice you eat gets us an hour's work, right?"

Peter looked askance at Louisa, but good humor twinkled in his eyes. "No problem! And who might you be? The dowager queen I've heard so much about?"

"I don't know about that." Louisa sniffed as she sent Peter a suspicious look. "But you don't look too strong," she snorted, giving him the once over.

"Mrs. Haymaker—you just have to be Mrs. Haymaker—what I lack in strength I make up for with stamina. Tell me what you think at five o'clock."

"You bet I will!"

Peter smiled. "I'm sure of it! Oh, and you might want to get another pot of coffee going because there's people coming from all over. The whole valley is talking about what's going on here in Primrose. *The Revival*, they're calling it." Peter laughed when the women stood there all agog. "What's the matter, girls? You *did* want to get this market off the ground, didn't you?"

"Yes, but—"

"Well, then… Hey, Ms. Jody, want to cut me up some of that blueberry pie, get my engines going?"

"No pie till tonight, Messer! But I'll set aside a slice *just for you*." She winked.

"Good girl—" Peter smiled "—because I plan to stick around a while."

Sitting high on his tractor, his eyes hidden by his hat, Rafe observed Peter's arrival with a long hard stare and clenched jaw. He didn't miss a beat when Peter waved hello, which he pretended not to see. Messer was a nice guy, sure, but Rafe viewed him as an intrusion. He even found the doctor's goodwill a shade irritating. Unintentionally or not, Peter cast doubts on Rafe's ability to win Maggie over, and his presence today could only mean one thing: he was campaigning for Maggie's affection. Messer would have an easy time of it, too, the way Maggie was acting. Rafe almost growled.

He stayed on the tractor instead, far longer than he intended, the rest of the afternoon, in fact. He had only been planning to stay an hour, to make sure everyone understood he wasn't against the farmer's market, and to assure himself that the cleanup did not incur any environmental damage. Not that it wasn't a sight for sore eyes, but he'd had a nightmare vision of someone cutting down the oaks that bordered the square, that were almost a landmark, they were so old. Thankfully, that didn't seem to be part of the plan. But with Peter Messer wandering about, waving his damned coffee cup and shaking everybody's hand as if he were a damned politician, Rafe could not bring himself to get down from the tractor. He would have to talk to Peter if he did, make nice, when he felt just the opposite.

Unsure what to do, Rafe remained in his seat so that by five o'clock he had leveled a field that was so flat it could have been tarred. Only the dinner bell, rung enthusiastically by his own son, prompted him to turn off the engine. Heading over to the makeshift wash stand, he sluiced his grimy head with water. The cool water made him feel almost human, so that when Peter handed him a towel, Rafe was almost civil.

"Thanks."

"You're welcome. I was wondering when you were going to get down from that tractor. Your neighbors are suitably impressed. It seems they weren't expecting you."

"You know how it is," Rafe said, toweling his hair.

"Sure thing," Peter said agreeably. "I met your son, Amos, by the way. He's a great kid."

"Thanks."

"He told me he wants to be a doctor when he grows up."

"Sure he does." Rafe frowned as he tossed the towel aside. "After he takes the gold at the Olympics, graduates college, goes to veterinary school, and beats me at chess."

"In no particular order, I'd imagine." Peter laughed as he walked with Rafe to the picnic tables.

"Hey, Rafe," Frank called as he saw Rafe and Peter approach. "Come sit down, man. You could probably eat a wolf the way you've been riding that tractor all day."

"I could," Rafe agreed solemnly. "That whole platter of chicken, for starters."

"Soaked overnight in buttermilk and fried just the way you like it," Louisa promised, "so step this way, Burnside, and sit yourself down. I set this place just for you."

Right beside Maggie, Rafe was happy to see, although Maggie was so busy handing round platters of food that she didn't notice him till he took his seat. He missed the satisfied glint in Louisa's eye as she handed him the chicken, and the look of triumph she sent Peter Messer. But Peter saw it and laughed.

"What?" asked Jody, sitting beside Peter.

"Oh, nothing." Peter grinned. "Just enjoying the comedy of errors."

Dinner went on till well past dusk. It was just too delightful to sit out on the newly cut lawn, breathe in the sweet smell of fresh-cut grass, enjoy the rare company of neighbors on a balmy summer night while their children ran around the square. School was just around the corner, in three days, and the kids knew it. The light sweaters the women wore hinted, too, at the coming change of season. Maggie hadn't bothered with her sweater, though, and every brush of her bare arm against Rafe's elbow was divine torture to him. Almost he could smell the afternoon sun on her skin, admired the golden glow on her face (when he dared to look), delighted in the sound of her laughter as she joked with the table. Was anyone ever so close to heaven, he wondered, and yet so tormented? Because sitting next to Maggie, when all he wanted to do was take her in his arms, seemed to be the very seat of hell.

Not that she spoke to him much. *Pass the salt, please*, or, *Would you like more lemonade?* was all she spared him. He glanced over at Peter Messer to see how he was handling Rafe's proximity to Maggie, but Peter seemed undisturbed. He was fully occupied, politely entertaining Jody, which Rafe had to admit was very civil of the man considering he probably wanted to be sitting next to Maggie.

Wait, then! The thought suddenly occurred to Rafe that maybe Maggie would have preferred to sit next to Messer. It had never occurred to him until that moment that he might be an obstacle to her happiness. Watching her, then watching Peter, he could detect no undertones, but the way Peter suddenly caught his eye and grinned sent Rafe in a tailspin. Was Peter sending him a message? The way he smiled…it wasn't quite a smile…more like a smirk. *Was it a smirk?* Rafe was so confused he didn't know what to think. If a man truly loved a woman, only her happiness mattered, right? But what if her happiness was with another man? And what if you weren't feeling so noble?

And why was Peter looking at him so weirdly? That damned look on his face…the way he stared… He was *definitely* trying to tell Rafe something, but what? *To stay away from Maggie?* Damn! Why didn't Messer pay more attention to Jody? Just look at that poor girl! Anyone could tell she was crazy about him. Boy, was she being taken for some ride! Perhaps Rafe should tell her that Peter had his eye on Maggie. Oh, sure, and be shot for the messenger. Thanks, but no thanks. Not when it was Peter Messer who should be shot!

Maybe that was it! Maybe he should have it out with Messer, tell him that Maggie was his.

But Maggie *wasn't* his, Rafe thought sadly. Just listen to the way she laughed at Peter's jokes. Just look how she smiled at Messer, even from a distance. No, Maggie most certainly wasn't his.

Chapter Fourteen

Rafe rooted about his farm for three weeks before he started getting on his own nerves. Every morning, he drove Amos down the mountain to school, then drove straight back up the mountain to tend his orchards. He told himself that the harvest was fast approaching— he had actually already begun picking apples—but the truth was, he was in hiding. He had been so traumatized by the events of Labor Day that he had no energy to confront either Maggie or Peter or himself. It was easier to let things ride, let nature take its course, even if nature was heading down the wrong road.

Louisa called, but when she began to berate him for hiding out, Rafe told her he had an emergency and had to go. *Click*.

Friends called to find out what was up, but if they got too personal, he was curt to the point of rudeness. Hearing the phone click, they backed off, figuring Rafe was just being Rafe.

Even Jody called to say hello, concerned about his disappearance. Rafe was courteous to *her*. He said he wanted to…could they…would she be… His half finished sentences confused her, but in the end he would not explain himself. *Click*.

When Jody mentioned the phone call to Peter, he only smiled, kissed the tip of her nose and said to give the poor fool time. He would not explain himself, either.

It was fate that brought Rafe and Peter Messer together the second week of October. Frank Congreve had called to ask Rafe if he would donate some apples to the farmer's market. It was about to open for the first time on Saturday and they were soliciting donations. Rafe promised him two crates and agreed to drop them off at the square around seven, Saturday morning. Rafe figured if he got there at six he could leave them under a tree and hightail it back home before he saw Maggie, and it would have happened that way, too, except that Peter spotted him before Rafe could make his getaway.

"Hey, Rafe," he said, giving him a jovial back slap. "Long time no see." Grabbing a crate of apples, he trailed Rafe over to the table Frank was arranging.

"Hey, Rafe, good to see you could make it," Frank Congreve greeted him. "You can set those baskets right here on my table. *Jonahgolds,* aren't they? Thanks, Rafe. They're real beauties. They'll sell, all right, and fast, too."

Frank motioned over his shoulder to the dozen crates and baskets filled with a variety of fruits and vegetables waiting to be displayed. "I sure hope all this produce bodes well for the success of the market, or there are going to be some very disappointed people at the party tonight."

"We'll just have to eat the leftovers," Peter said philosophically.

"Messer, is food all you ever think about?"

"What can I say. I'm a gourmand—or is it gourmet? Whatever! A dyed-in-the-wool foodie." He grinned.

Frank chuckled. "Well, that's as may be, as long as you intend to *buy* some of this stuff."

"Not to worry, Frank, I brought plenty of cash. I was planning to shop, no matter what. Hey, Rafe, remember that shortbread I made when you visited? I'm selling some, so don't forget to stop by my table and buy a pound or two."

"I can't. I'm getting a delivery today and I don't know when it's arriving."

"Oh, come on, Rafe! *Today* of all days?"

"It's that horse I bought for Amos," Rafe said defensively.

Frank smiled. "Is that why you brought him over for a sleepover, last night?"

"It's a surprise."

"Lucky kid. Too bad it has to be today, though."

"It just worked out that way," Rafe said absently, as he scanned the faces of the crowd building, nervous to run into Maggie. "Well, so…I guess I'll be going, then…"

"If you must," Frank said as he set another basket on the table. "But, hey, I almost forgot. You *are* going to the party tonight, aren't you?"

"What party?" Rafe asked uneasily.

"The First Annual Celebration of the Primrose Farmer's Market, over at Hendersen's barn. Six o'clock. It's a combination pot luck dinner and dance. You can pick Amos up there."

"I was hoping you could drop him off. I thought maybe you and the boys might like to see his new horse."

"Sorry, but I'm sure that Fannie is going to be too bushed to want to do anything but go home. She was up most of the night with Maggie and Jody and Louisa, baking pies. They were just pulling the last ones from the oven when I left."

"Besides," Peter added, "you can congratulate me and my girl. We've decided to get *pre-engaged.*"

My girl? Pre-engaged? Rafe could hardly breathe must less speak. "What…does…*pre-engaged*… mean?"

"It means that we've decided to date each other…exclusively. The dating part wasn't too hard, but convincing her about the exclusively part was a bit of a chore. So I expect to see you tonight. This is way too important for you to not be there, especially since you were there when we first met.

Maggie would be pretty upset, too, if you didn't show. Hey, you know what? If we ever get married, you have to be my best man."

Rafe frowned. "I thought you said you were only dating."

"I know, I know." Peter grinned. "But give me a year. I guarantee you'll be hearing wedding bells all over the mountain."

Rafe didn't care if he never heard wedding bells again in his life, and to hear Maggie's and Peter's would be the worst. He was so angry and frustrated, he went home and picked clean four apple trees before the afternoon was done. By the time Mr. Fry had delivered Amos's horse, Rafe was exhausted. He was so hot and dirty and sweaty after he'd settled the palomino in the barn that he had to stand in the shower for ten minutes while hot water sluiced down his body and soothed his aching muscles. He only left because the water ran cold.

He didn't want to attend the party, he really and truly did not, and tried every which way he could to think up an excuse not to attend. In the end, he knew that he must show his face, but decided it would only be for the time it could take to say that he was there. So at six-thirty, freshly shaved and badly nicked, he steeled himself for the worst.

Driving up to the Hendersens', he saw the barn lit up, festive white icicle lights dripping from the roof. It looked to him like the whole town was there, standing outside on the lawn, spilling out of the doorway, and when he peeked, filling the brightly lit barn. Rafe greeted the small band of men standing just beyond the light. Beers in hand, it was a jovial group that returned his greeting. From inside the barn, the sound of fiddles reached his ears. The cheerful music told him that the market must have gone well, and his friends confirmed its huge success. Maybe they *were* on the right track to the revival Peter Messer spoke of. Lord knew the town deserved it, and part of him was proud of the accomplishment they were celebrating. He just wished he could share it with them, but that wasn't possible for a man with a broken heart.

"Hey, Rafe," Frank called, stepping from the shadows to hand Rafe a beer.

"Hey, Frank." Rafe declined the beer politely. "Sorry, I'm driving tonight."

"But not too soon, I hope." Frank smiled.

"Soon enough. The horse came and I want to give it to Amos before he's exhausted. I assume he's inside?" he asked, peering over Frank's shoulder.

"Having a ball. Everyone who sold at the market is here, and even some who helped us set up, last Labor Day. You should have seen it, Rafe. People came from all over. We almost didn't have enough parking space. Got to get back on that tractor, Mr. Burnside, and clear us another lot. Of course, we don't expect it will be that crowded *every* weekend. I think a lot of people came out of curiosity and to lend their support. And they sure did. Wasn't a pie left by ten o'clock. You should have seen the girls' faces. They didn't know whether to laugh or cry.

They'll be baking up another storm, next week, I can promise you. They're talking a regular production line, mail orders and everything."

Rafe was genuinely surprised. He had expected the market to be a modest success, nothing as spectacular as Frank had just described. "Wow! That's terrific."

"It sure is," Frank said proudly. "Now they're forming a committee to decide how to *spend* the money! I told Fannie she was just figuring a way out of the house for an evening." Frank winked. "Not that she doesn't deserve it."

"Well, it's good to hear the market went well. So, okay, I guess I'll go find Amos, see what the boy is up to."

"Don't forget to eat something," Frank called after him. "Fannie brought a whole platter of ribs and a bucket of potato salad, although with this crowd, who knows what's left."

Rafe nodded but said nothing. He had no intention of walking into that barn if he could avoid it. As for eating, he couldn't put a morsel in his mouth, his throat was so tight. Maybe it would be best if he walked around to the back of the barn, see if he could spot Amos from the rear door.

Swerving abruptly, Rafe disappeared into the shadows. Wondering at some rustling in the bushes, he was amused to see a young couple wrapped in each other's arms. Stolen kisses. Young love. Poor fools.

Not like him, a bitter thread of despair piercing his heart as he thought about Maggie, how he had lost her to Peter. How much he had lost to Peter, *beyond* the lonely night that loomed, *beyond* the future of many lonely nights.

Standing in the shadows, leaning against the door, watching Maggie and Peter dance, he knew that nothing would satisfy his broken heart. Watching her sway, he felt a churning in his belly, and understood for the first time what he had been hard put to admit, that he had been looking forward to making Maggie a part of his life. He wanted more than to make love to her, he wanted to wake with her, breakfast together, argue—and make up! Maggie had reminded him of the simple pleasure of being alive, having friends… having a woman to call his own. So much so that, now, as he watched her dance with Peter Messer, he understood in full measure what he had lost.

Amos would be grown soon, he was already spending nights away, and Rafe must let him go. The boy had his own life to lead. But God, it would be so quiet in the house. And all the horses and dogs and the exhaustion of his field work would not make up for a dinner table set for one.

"Hi, Dad. Hey, why are you standing here in the dark?"

Startled from his reverie, Rafe looked down to see his son tugging on his sleeve.

"Hey, Amos. I was looking for you. Ready to go?"

"It's kind of early. Don't you want to go inside and eat something? Louisa makes the best fried chicken in the world."

Rafe smiled. "She does, doesn't she? Maybe we

could get the recipe. But I'd really like to leave now. I've got to be up early."

"But, Dad, it's a party!"

Rafe almost relented until he thought about the horse waiting to meet for his new master. He had a hunch it was going to be impossible to put Amos to bed once he saw his present, much less wake him in the morning. Extra chores for me tomorrow, Rafe sighed. But it would be worth it to see Amos' face when he saw the horse.

"Come on, son, let's go home," Rafe said, as he headed for his truck. Jingling his car keys, he turned his back on his future.

Rafe was right. Once Amos spotted the horse waiting for him in the corral, there was no sleep for either of them. Rafe didn't mind. Feeling low, he found it a very precious thing to be able to share the evening with his son. The boy had been campaigning for months to have a horse, and Rafe knew his son never had any real hope of getting his wish. So Amos had been ecstatic when he saw the horse standing in the stall.

After much begging, Amos finally convinced his father to let him lead the horse to the corral. Watching his son gentle the horse, nuzzle its neck, feed it sugar cubes, Rafe was glad he'd caved in, and knew this was a moment that would not repeat itself. And then, Amos refused to go to bed until he named it. After much discussion and laughter, standing in the twilight as the moon rose, Amos settled on a name. *Star*.

"Star is showing off, isn't he?" Amos laughed as he watched his horse gallop around the corral.

"Horses do that," Rafe smiled. "Kids, people… Human nature, I guess."

"I suppose," Amos agreed. Enjoying the antics of Star, they stood, shoulder to shoulder, talking aimlessly as it got dark.

"Do you think she'll get along with Tylla?"

"Asolutely. They're kindred spirits."

Rafe's answer seemed to satisfy Amos. Thoughtfully, they watched Star gallop about.

"You should have come to the market today, Dad," Amos said absently. "You should have seen the crowd. I haven't seen that many people *ever,* not even when Maggie took us to the mall. It was amazing!"

"Well, now you know where I was. Waiting here for Star to arrive. I didn't want to tell you and spoil your surprise."

Perched on the fence, Amos nodded.

"Anyway, Frank told me it was a big success," Rafe said, offhandedly.

"It sure was, except for when Fannie burst into tears because everyone kept asking her for pies but they ran out and she didn't have any more to sell and Maggie said she couldn't believe it they would have made *so much money* and Jody said *who knew* and Louisa said *she did* and that would teach them all a lesson not to wait till the last minute and—"

"Whoa there, boy, slow down!" Rafe smiled.

Amos grinned. "Maggie tells me I talk too much, too. She says I'd make a good politician."

Rafe ruffled his son's hair. "She may be right."

"She was looking for you all day."

"Is that right?" Rafe asked, trying not to appear too interested.

"Yup. I heard her ask Fannie a million times if you were coming. But Fannie said she didn't know, so I told Maggie that you never came to parties. She looked kind of sad. I think she likes you, Dad."

"You think so? Well, that's of no account, now."

"Why? Don't you like Maggie? When she took us out for pizza that time, I thought you liked her a whole lot."

"I did. I do. But now that she's seeing that Messer fellow, she won't have time for...us."

"Seeing Dr. Messer? You mean like in *dating?* Oh," Amos said thoughtfully.

"That's how it is."

"But I thought he was in love with Jody," Amos said, thoroughly confused. "When I saw them kissing, I thought—"

Rafe tried to stay calm. "When you saw who kissing who, son?"

"Peter and Jody!"

"Are you sure?"

"Of course I'm sure!"

"When did you see them kissing, son?"

"Tonight, at the Hendersens'. They were standing in the back field holding hands and talking, and then he kissed her. They didn't see me, but I could see them, and I could tell she didn't like it at first, the way she was squirming, but she didn't push him away so I guess she liked it, after all."

Rafe was livid. No way was Peter Messer going to betray Maggie and play both women for fools.

"Son, you know what? I forgot to get my apple baskets back from Frank. What say we drive back to the Hendersens' and get them back? I'll be needing them in the morning."

"Sure thing," Amos cried, jumping down from the fence to lead Star back to his stall. "Then I can tell everyone about Star."

All the while they drove back down the mountain, Rafe told himself he should be calm, but he was so angry at Peter, and so worried about Maggie, that he could hardly think straight. The main thing he knew was to not hurt Maggie. The main thing was to hurt Peter Messer! But a public spectacle would embarrass Maggie. Jody, as well, come to think if it. Jody was a part of this triangle, too, and was going to be hurt also, no matter how this nasty scene played out. How then, to proceed? The thing to probably do was get Messer alone and give him a good thrashing. That would ensure Peter's banishment from Primrose, and that at least would protect the women from his sweet-talking ways. Then they would only run into Messer when they left town, more of a problem for Maggie since they worked in the same field, less of a problem for Jody, who would soon be returning to Boston. Tomorrow, probably, when she learned about Messer's two-timing ways.

By the time the Burnsides pulled up to the Hendersen farm, Amos was sprawled out, fast asleep on the front seat. It was just as well, Rafe thought grimly,

as he climbed down from his truck. He would rather
Amos didn't witness his temper. He had a hell of a
temper when riled up, and he was definitely riled up
now.

Retracing his steps of an hour before, Rafe searched
for Peter Messer, but the doctor was nowhere in sight.
Maggie was, though, standing at the dessert table with
Louisa Haymaker, laughing and sipping punch.

Peering past Maggie's shoulder, Louisa eyed him
up and down with a curious squint. "My, my, will
you just look what the cat dragged in."

Turning, Maggie's eyes widened when she saw
who it was. "Rafe! I'm so glad you could make it!
Amos said you didn't go to parties, but I was hoping
you'd make an exception, it's such a special night."

Tipping his hat, Rafe smiled weakly. "Yes, he
told me the market was a huge success."

"Was it ever!" she said with a broad smile that
made his heart flip.

A pity, he thought, that Louisa was not so easily
pleased with him.

"Didn't I see you here earlier tonight?" she
asked bluntly.

"I stopped by to get Amos."

"Oh, right. Well, why'd you come back, then?"

"I forgot something."

"Yes, you did," Maggie teased him. "You forgot
to ask me to dance."

"You want to dance with *me?*" Rafe asked, surprised.

Maggie blushed. "I was hoping that we might

call a truce, at least for tonight. The market was such a splendid success, Rafe, that *everyone* ought to be celebrating!"

"I don't dance," Rafe said in a clipped voice.

"Oh. Okay," Maggie faltered. "It was just a thought."

But Rafe saw Louisa roll her eyes in time to realize his mistake.

"But if I did, I would," he added quickly.

Maggie brightened. "You would? Would you like to try now?"

Rafe looked around at the dancers whirling around the barn, kicking up straw and having the time of their lives. No way was he going to embarrass himself. His errand was hard enough without playing the gallant. "Have you seen Peter Messer?"

Disappointed, Maggie shrugged. "He was just here a minute ago. He was dancing with Jody."

Rafe peered into the crowd. "If you'll excuse me, then, I'll go find him. I have something to…say…to him…important…" he mumbled, and with a tip of his hat, he was gone.

"Sure," Maggie said, as she watched Rafe disappear into the crowd. "No problem."

Louisa stared thoughtfully after Rafe. "Maggie, I smell trouble. If I were you, I'd go after that man and see what's up. He has a mean look in his eye that might not bode well for Messer."

Maggie frowned. "You think?"

"I do!"

Maggie watched Rafe hurry from the barn.

"Could be you're right. If I'm not back in thirty minutes, send for reinforcements."

Following Rafe, Maggie left the barn to find it was nightfall, and beyond the vicinity of the barn, the shadows were deep. It was a little spooky searching in the dark for signs of life. Hearing voices on the air, she had to force herself to track the low murmurings into the woods, and it was a relief to find Rafe and Peter and Jody talking by one of Hendersen's tool sheds. The lone, dangling bulb gave off so little light that it was hard to see her friends' faces, but their voices told her everything she needed to know. This was a *heated* discussion.

"Jeezus, Rafe," she heard Peter shouting, "if you would just listen—"

Maggie lost the rest of his sentence, but not the gist.

"Messer, I don't want to hear *anything* a lowlife like you has to say!"

Was Rafe actually *growling?*

"Boy, Rafe, are you ever one pig-headed son of a gun!"

So, Jody was adding her two cents, too!

"Damn it, Jody, stay out of this! You have no idea—"

"*Damn you,* Rafe, I most certainly do!"

"Damn it, Jody, you don't! All I'm doing is trying to save you from this two-timing lowlife! That man is pond scum!"

"Pond scum?" Peter bellowed, incredulous. "Why, you—"

"Rafe! Jody! Peter!" Maggie's voice was a commanding fury as she stepped into the light. The three combatants turned as one.

"Maggie! Oh, you have no idea how happy I am to see you," Jody cried, waving her crutch as she hobbled over to her friend. "Maybe *you* can talk some sense into this nutcase."

"Stay out of this, Maggie," Rafe charged her. "Jody has no idea what she's talking about."

"She's not the only one." Peter snarled.

Rafe's hands turned to fists. Reading his intention, Peter put up his own fists. But as suddenly, he started to laugh. "Jeezus, Rafe, come on! You aren't *really* going to hit me, are you? This is ridiculous!"

"You think so?" Rafe was so angry he took hold of Peter's shirt, balling it in his fist.

Peter tried to push Rafe away, but he was laughing so hard he could hardly contain himself.

And suddenly Maggie understood everything. "Rafe," she said quietly, "let Peter go."

But Rafe was frozen in time.

"Rafe, *let him go!* Jody, take your boyfriend inside and let me talk to Rafe."

Boyfriend?

Rafe faltered.

"That's right, Rafe. Peter is Jody's *boyfriend*. Now, one last time. Let him go."

Rafe's hands dropped like he'd been holding hot coals. He even wiped his hands on his jeans.

Peter's mouth quirked with wry, good humor. "You know, I think—"

"Peter!"

Peter raised his hands, palms out. "Okay, okay. Lotsa luck, Doc. You're going to need it."

Maggie and Rafe watched as Peter and Jody returned to the party, then Maggie turned to Rafe, her hands on her hips, her eyes flashing thunderbolts. "What the hell were you thinking?" she hissed.

"I—"

"That's right! You weren't!"

"I—"

"Of all the confounded, embarrassing and stupid—*stupid!*—things to do."

"I—"

"Did you think that behaving like a Neanderthal was going to solve anything? How could you even *think* that Peter and I—" Maggie could hardly bear to finish her sentence. "That Peter and I— Haven't you seen him around Jody? Rafe Burnside, are you blind, besides dumb?"

"Maggie, I—"

"Oh, for heaven's sake, can't you say anything but *I?*"

Rafe looked chagrined. "But I—"

Maggie looked at Rafe like he had sprouted horns. Shaking her head, she could barely keep from doing to him what he had been about to do to Peter. "Oh, Rafe, I could just strangle you!"

Totally frustrated, Rafe seized Maggie by the shoulders and pulled her into his arms. "Maggie, please shut up! We both talk too much!" To a man of few words, action was better. His mouth pressed to hers was a whole conversation.

"Rafe." Maggie's voice was a weak sigh when he finally let her go, minutes later.

"Maggie," he said, his forehead pressed to hers. "I can't go on like this. I'm crazy head-over-heels in love with you and it's making me act like a lunatic. Jesus Christ, I can't believe I was just about to beat the living daylights out of Messer! I can't think straight, I can't sleep, and I haven't been able to do either one since you came to town. And the worst, my son is asleep in my damned truck when he should be home in bed—*and it's all your fault!*"

"What?" Maggie gasped. "Are you're blaming *me?*"

"Maggie, marry me! I'm begging you!" Rafe begged, his voice entreating.

"So you can get back to your trees?" Maggie accused him, her own voice mocking.

"*Exactly.* So that I can get back to my trees. So that at the end of the day, when I come home, you'll be standing on the porch, pretty as a picture, and waiting for me with a cold beer."

"Oh, *that's* not going to happen, cowboy. I have a job, too, remember."

"Right. Sorry, I forgot. So, I'll be waiting for *you,* then, on the porch, when you get home."

"With a cold beer?" Maggie asked, faintly amused.

"Iced tea, if you prefer." Rafe smiled, kissing her softly on the lips.

"That's better. What else?"

"Dinner?" He hesitated.

"If you make it." She grinned.

"If you like frozen food, I'll make it."

"Hey, what about that wonderful Scotch broth you made?"

Rafe laughed. "Oh, *that.* That was special. It took me hours to make it. I did it for you. I'm a big fan of bologna sandwiches."

"Ugh! Seems like we have some negotiating to do."

"Maggie, will you consider it, seriously? You must know by now that I love you."

A finger pressed to her lips, Maggie thought for a moment.

"I suppose I *do* have my reputation to think about..."

"There is that." Rafe smiled faintly.

"You haven't asked about my feelings for *you.*"

Rafe frowned. "The way I figure it, if you say *yes,* then you love me. You aren't the type to be with a man you don't love."

Maggie smiled. "Too true. Okay, I'll give it a try."

Rafe shook his head. "Sorry, no try outs, Maggie. This is a one-shot deal. But don't worry, I'll make you happy."

"And are you so sure I'll make *you* happy?"

"Do you snore?" Rafe teased.

"No!" Maggie laughed. "Do you?"

"You'll have to find that out for yourself, sweetheart."

Matters settled to both parties' satisfaction, Rafe took her hand and kissed it. "I'd love to stay and continue this conversation, sweetheart, but there's a little boy asleep in my truck who ought to be home in his bed."

Maggie looked up at Rafe, her eyes shining. "I'll have a lot more time with Amos," she mused.

"He's been waiting a long time for this."

"You think?"

"*I know*. Since the day Rose left. And since the day *you* arrived. He's been courting you for me. Or courting me for you. I don't know which, but he's sure going to be one hell of a happy kid when he wakes up tomorrow. Almost as happy as his dad."

Epilogue

"Okay everyone," Fanny Congreve shouted, having enormous fun banging out a staccato call for attention with the mallet her husband had carved her. "Let's have a little quiet here."

Maggie saw Fannie cast a confident smile at Frank. She sure had come a long way from the pale wisp Maggie had met on her first trip up the mountain. Had it only been six months ago? And her boys, grown so much the past winter. Sitting beside their dad in the front row, freshly scrubbed, their hair neatly combed. Silent beneath their father's quiet gaze. No doubt Frank had read his kids the riot act on the way over to the meeting. *No,* Frank didn't have to do any such thing, Maggie realized quickly.

They adored their pa, and dared not disobey him. A quick meaningful glance from Frank always brought them to attention. Obedience borne of respect, not fear. The desire to make him proud was deeply ingrained in each of those little boys. Idly, Maggie wondered if such a thing could be bottled.

Looking out over the sea over heads in front of her, she smiled. Anyone who could manage the trip over the mountain was there. Snow threatened, but it would do so for many months to come. No matter. Hardly anything was cancelled in the mountains due to weather. There were tons of things to do before spring came, many matters to attend to, if Primrose was to emerge whole from its chrysalis, and Maggie had a hunch that snow would not stop it.

Glancing at Rafe, sitting beside Fannie up on the school stage, Maggie nodded her amazement. Both of them spruced up, Fannie wearing a new wool dress that became her, while, wonder of wonders, Rafe had agreed to allow Maggie to cut his hair. Not the greatest job, she had laughed the night before, the way he kept burying his face in her breasts while she wielded a pair of long scissors. *You, sir, are interfering with progress*, she had warned him. *She hoped he liked the shaggy look!* He hadn't cared, and so he had proved as he coaxed her toward the bedroom.

He was their spokesman now, an idea that Rafe had resisted but wore well, once he had understood the need. He was the lynch pin on which everything rested, even if Fannie Congreve wielded the hammer—and so his neighbors told him the night they came knocking on his door. *Primrose needed a steady hand to point the way…he was the one they most trusted…people would listen to him…would he give it a try?*

Beside her, Amos wriggled, tired from his long day, but Maggie had insisted he attend the meeting. She wanted him to see what his dad was doing, how important it was to Primrose. Hopefully, one day, Amos would be sitting up there, helping *his* neighbors along, just like his dad was doing now. If Primrose could become the kind of town that would make a kid want to stay. A young man, rather, she corrected herself wryly. But not too soon, she hoped, as Amos fell asleep on her lap.

"…as to the matter of the farmer's market… amazing profit…" she heard Fannie's thin voice grow stronger as she spoke. Glancing at Rafe, she found him staring straight at her with his piercing, dark look. Even though she had hidden herself in the back of the audience, bundled beneath a thick scarf and wooly hat he had found her. No one could tell that he was smiling, he had that kind of face, but *she* knew he was. She knew every inch of his beautiful body, knew exactly what pleasured her husband, the taste of his mouth, the feel of his hands.

Knew, too, how much it had cost him to be sitting up there, hating the notoriety, but doing it for her, and for the town that was staggering to its feet after so many lean years. Not that anything would happen overnight. There were long years ahead, for both the town and for Maggie and Rafe. But they would manage…in concert…as one…as a family. Together.

* * * * *

For a sneak preview of Marie Ferrarella's
DOCTOR IN THE HOUSE,
coming to NEXT in September,
please turn the page.

He didn't look like an unholy terror.

But maybe that reputation was exaggerated, Bailey DelMonico thought as she turned in her chair to look toward the doorway.

The man didn't seem scary at all.

Dr. Munro, or Ivan the Terrible, was tall, with an athletic build and wide shoulders. The cheekbones beneath what she estimated to be day-old stubble were prominent. His hair was light brown and just this side of unruly. Munro's hair looked as if he used his fingers for a comb and didn't care who knew it.

The eyes were brown, almost black as they were aimed at her. There was no other word for it. Aimed. As if he was debating whether or not to fire at point-blank range.

Somewhere in the back of her mind, a line from a B movie, "Be afraid—be very afraid…" whispered along the perimeter of her brain. Warning her. Almost against her will, it caused her to brace her shoulders. Bailey had to remind herself to breathe in and out like a normal person.

The chief of staff, Dr. Bennett, had tried his level

best to put her at ease and had almost succeeded. But an air of tension had entered with Munro. She wondered if Dr. Bennett was bracing himself as well, bracing for some kind of disaster or explosion.

"Ah, here he is now," Harold Bennett announced needlessly. The smile on his lips was slightly forced, and the look in his gray, kindly eyes held a warning as he looked at his chief neurosurgeon. "We were just talking about you, Dr. Munro."

"Can't imagine why," Ivan replied dryly.

Harold cleared his throat, as if that would cover the less than friendly tone of voice Ivan had just displayed. "Dr. Munro, this is the young woman I was telling you about yesterday."

Now his eyes dissected her. Bailey felt as if she was undergoing a scalpel-less autopsy right then and there. "Ah yes, the Stanford Special."

He made her sound like something that was listed at the top of a third-rate diner menu. There was enough contempt in his voice to offend an entire delegation from the UN.

Summoning the bravado that her parents always claimed had been infused in her since the moment she first drew breath, Bailey put out her hand. "Hello. I'm Dr. Bailey DelMonico."

Ivan made no effort to take the hand offered to him. Instead, he slid his long, lanky form bonelessly into the chair beside her. He proceeded to move the chair ever so slightly so that there was even more space between them. Ivan faced the chief of staff, but the words he spoke were addressed to her.

"You're a doctor, DelMonico, when I say you're a doctor," he informed her coldly, sparing her only one frosty glance to punctuate the end of his statement.

Harold stifled a sigh. "Dr. Munro is going to take over your education. Dr. Munro—" he fixed Ivan with a steely gaze that had been known to send lesser doctors running for their antacids, but, as always, seemed to have no effect on the chief neurosurgeon "—I want you to award her every consideration. From now on, Dr. DelMonico is to be your shadow, your sponge and your assistant." He emphasized the last word as his eyes locked with Ivan's. "Do I make myself clear?"

For his part, Ivan seemed completely unfazed. He merely nodded, his eyes and expression unreadable. "Perfectly."

His hand was on the doorknob. Bailey sprang to her feet. Her chair made a scraping noise as she moved it back and then quickly joined the neurosurgeon before he could leave the office.

Closing the door behind him, Ivan leaned over and whispered into her ear, "Just so you know, I'm going to be your worst nightmare."

Bailey DelMonico has finally
gotten her life on track, and is
passionate about her recent career
change. Nothing will stand in the way
of her becoming a doctor...that is,
until she's paired with the sharp-tongued
Dr. Ivan Munro.

Watch the sparks fly in

Doctor in
the House

by *USA TODAY* Bestselling Author
Marie Ferrarella

Available September 2007

Intrigued? Read more at
TheNextNovel.com

HARLEQUIN®
Next™

HN88141

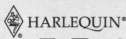

HARLEQUIN®

NeXt™

GET $1.⁰⁰ OFF

your purchase of any
Harlequin NEXT novel.

Receive $1.⁰⁰ off

any Harlequin NEXT novel.

*Available wherever books are sold, including
most bookstores, supermarkets, drugstores
and discount stores.*

Coupon expires February 28, 2008.
Redeemable at participating retail outlets
in the U.S. only. Limit one coupon per customer.

5 65373 00076 2   (8100)0 11436

HNCPNSSEUS09

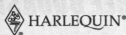

HARLEQUIN®

NeXt™

GET $1.⁰⁰ OFF

your purchase of any
Harlequin NEXT novel.

Receive $1.⁰⁰ off

any Harlequin NEXT novel.

*Available wherever books are sold, including
most bookstores, supermarkets, drugstores
and discount stores.*

Coupon expires February 28, 2008.
Redeemable at participating retail outlets
in Canada only. Limit one coupon per customer.

RETAILER: Harlequin Enterprises Ltd. will pay the face value of this coupon plus 10.25 cents
if submitted by customer for this specified product only. Any other use constitutes fraud. Coupon is
nonassignable. Void if taxed, prohibited or restricted by law. Consumer must pay any government taxes.
Mail to Harlequin Enterprises Ltd., P.O. Box 3000, Saint John, New Brunswick E2L 4L3, Canada. Limit
one coupon per customer. Valid in Canada only.

52608041

REQUEST YOUR FREE BOOKS!
2 FREE NOVELS PLUS 2 FREE GIFTS!

SPECIAL EDITION®
Life, Love and Family!

YES! Please send me 2 FREE Silhouette Special Edition® novels and my 2 FREE gifts. After receiving them, if I don't wish to receive any more books, I can return the shipping statement marked "cancel." If I don't cancel, I will receive 6 brand-new novels every month and be billed just $4.24 per book in the U.S., or $4.99 per book in Canada, plus 25¢ shipping and handling per book and applicable taxes, if any*. That's a savings of at least 15% off the cover price! I understand that accepting the 2 free books and gifts places me under no obligation to buy anything. I can always return a shipment and cancel at any time. Even if I never buy another book from Silhouette, the two free books and gifts are mine to keep forever. 235 SDN EEYU 335 SDN EEY6

Name	(PLEASE PRINT)

Address	Apt.

City	State/Prov.	Zip/Postal Code

Signature (if under 18, a parent or guardian must sign)

Mail to the **Silhouette Reader Service™:**
IN U.S.A.: P.O. Box 1867, Buffalo, NY 14240-1867
IN CANADA: P.O. Box 609, Fort Erie, Ontario L2A 5X3
Not valid to current Silhouette Special Edition subscribers.

Want to try two free books from another line?
Call 1-800-873-8635 or visit www.morefreebooks.com.

* Terms and prices subject to change without notice. NY residents add applicable sales tax. Canadian residents will be charged applicable provincial taxes and GST. This offer is limited to one order per household. All orders subject to approval. Credit or debit balances in a customer's account(s) may be offset by any other outstanding balance owed by or to the customer. Please allow 4 to 6 weeks for delivery.

Your Privacy: Silhouette is committed to protecting your privacy. Our Privacy Policy is available online at www.eHarlequin.com or upon request from the Reader Service. From time to time we make our lists of customers available to reputable firms who may have a product or service of interest to you. If you would prefer we not share your name and address, please check here. ☐

COMING NEXT MONTH

#1855 I DO! I DO!—Pamela Toth
Montana Mavericks: Striking It Rich
When it came to jobs and men, bartender Liz Stanton hadn't quite found her way. Then shy business owner Mitchell Cates stepped into the breach to kill two birds with one stone—offering Liz a foothold on the corporate ladder...and a chance at true love.

#1856 TAMING THE PLAYBOY—Marie Ferrarella
The Sons of Lily Moreau
Upon witnessing a brutal car accident, Dr. Georges Armand came to the rescue of Vienna Hellenbeck and her injured grandfather, a renowned pastry chef who offered Georges a lifetime supply of treats for his trouble. But it was Vienna who was the true delicacy. Did she have the secret ingredient to make the good doctor give up his playboy ways?

#1857 THE DADDY MAKEOVER—RaeAnne Thayne
The Women of Brambleberry House
It was just another day for Oregon Coast marine biologist Sage Benedetto—until she helped a little girl lost on the beach find her daddy, and life changed forever. For the daddy in question was multimillionaire hotelier Eben Spencer, who took an instant liking to this free-spirited naturalist and her outspoken ways...but was the feeling mutual?

#1858 RED WOLF'S RETURN—Mary J. Forbes
Since returning to Sweet Creek, wildlife artist Ethan Red Wolf had avoided his childhood love, Police Chief Meg McKee. But when he reported a crime on his property to Meg, a long-lost passion was rekindled with the sudden intensity of wildfire. Would her troubled teenage son and a painful secret tear her away from Ethan...again?

#1859 THE NEW GIRL IN TOWN—Brenda Harlen
After a serious illness stalled her career in fashion photography, Zoe Kozlowski was drifting...until a trip to Pinehurst, New York, brought her face-to-face with her dream home. The run-down Victorian needed work, and architect Mason Sullivan was the man for the job. But Mason was focused on a more enticing fixer-upper: Zoe's heart.

#1860 TO HAVE AND TO HOLD—Dawn Temple
Her grandfather's will was crystal clear: Lindy and Travis Monroe would have to reunite and live as husband and wife for a set period or she'd lose the family farm. Estranged since her miscarriage, they were skeptical of the setup but soon discovered that where there was a will, there was a way...to renew their vows for *all* time!

SSECNM0907